She should have pushed Dan away, explained that she was afraid of people, of getting close, of physical intimacy.

But she didn't.

As soon as Dan touched her, he realized an astounding paradox. The beautiful, alluring, sensuous woman in his arms seemed to have very little experience. He paused, pulled away slightly and looked down at her. She seemed to be relaxed and enjoying their closeness, but she was making no effort to encourage him. Was it possible that she didn't know how? He began to wonder if her amusing story might have some merit, after all. Where else but outer space would he find a woman with so many loving attributes so seemingly untouched?

She opened her eyes and stared up at him. When her gaze met his, she smiled a slow, enticing smile that caused a tightening deep within him. He'd never seen eyes like hers . . . they fascinated him, mesmerized him.

"I want to make love to you," he said huskily.

Dear Reader,

Welcome to Silhouette. Experience the magic of the wonderful world where two people fall in love. Meet heroines who will make you cheer for their happiness, and heroes (be they the boy next door or a handsome, mysterious stranger) who will win your heart. Silhouette Romances reflect the magic of love—sweeping you away with books that will make you laugh and cry, heartwarming, poignant stories that will move you time and time again.

In the next few months, we're publishing romances by many of your all-time favorites, such as Diana Palmer, Brittany Young, Emilie Richards and Arlene James. Your response to these authors and other authors of Silhouette Romances has served as a touchstone for us, and we're pleased to bring you more books with Silhouette's distinctive medley of charm, wit and—above all—*romance*.

I hope you enjoy this book and the many stories to come. Experience the magic!

Sincerely,

Tara Hughes
Senior Editor
Silhouette Books

ANNETTE BROADRICK
Strange Enchantment

Silhouette Romance

Published by Silhouette Books New York

America's Publisher of Contemporary Romance

This book is dedicated to Judy Talley,
whose daily encouragement kept me writing—
with my gratitude . . .

SILHOUETTE BOOKS
300 E. 42nd St., New York, N.Y. 10017

Copyright © 1987 by Annette Broadrick

ISBN: 0-373-08501-X

First Silhouette Books printing April 1987

America's Publisher of Contemporary Romance

Printed in the U.S.A.

ANNETTE BROADRICK

lives on the shores of The Lake of the Ozarks in Missouri, where she spends her time doing what she loves most—reading and writing romantic fiction. "For twenty-five years I lived in various large cities, working as a legal secretary, a very high-stress occcupation. I never thought I was capable of making a career change at this point in my life, but thanks to Silhouette I am now able to write full-time in the peaceful surroundings that have turned my life into a dream come true."

Had we but world enough, and time,
This coyness, lady, were no crime.
We would sit down, and think which way
To walk, and pass our long love's day.

Excerpted from "To His Coy Mistress,"
by Andrew Marvell (1621-1678)

ANNETTE BROADRICK

lives on the shores of The Lake of the Ozarks in Missouri, where she spends her time doing what she loves most—reading and writing romantic fiction. "For twenty-five years I lived in various large cities, working as a legal secretary, a very high-stress occcupation. I never thought I was capable of making a career change at this point in my life, but thanks to Silhouette I am now able to write full-time in the peaceful surroundings that have turned my life into a dream come true."

Had we but world enough, and time,
This coyness, lady, were no crime.
We would sit down, and think which way
To walk, and pass our long love's day.

Excerpted from "To His Coy Mistress,"
by Andrew Marvell (1621-1678)

Chapter One

*Y*our biggest problem, Elizabeth, is that you don't live here with the rest of us. You're off with your romantic English poets who have been dead for years, hiding away from today's world and all that's going on around you, refusing to face reality."

"That isn't true, Philip, I—"

"Of course it's true. We've known each other for seven years. Seven years, Elizabeth! It took me five years to convince you to marry me, and for the past two years you've refused to set a date. Yet you aren't honest enough to admit you don't love me so I can get on with my life."

"I do love you, Philip. It's only that—"

"That you're afraid of life, and of feelings and of being human. I know. I've tried to understand you, *because I love you. How many couples have been to-gether this long without ever making love? If I didn't love you, and continue to hope that you'd overcome your hesitancies, I would have walked away years ago. But I'm sick and tired of waiting, Elizabeth. Tired of pushing you, tired of watching for some sign that you're ready for me, willing to take an active part in our relationship. You don't seem to need or want me in your life and I no longer have the energy or desire to force a place for myself."*

"I can't seem to help it, Philip. It has nothing to do with the feelings I have for you. I really do love you."

"I don't believe you're capable of love, Elizabeth. You don't even understand what you've put me through. I can't take any more of this. I came over to-night to tell you that I'm ending our engagement. I want out."

"Oh, Philip, please don't feel this way. We can set a date. My classes will be over in six weeks. Maybe we can—"

"No. We can't. There is no more we, Elizabeth. As much as I love you, I can't take any more. Goodbye, Elizabeth."

A misty fog swirled and eddied between them as he turned away. He disappeared from view and she cried out. The scene shifted, and suddenly there was noise and confusion, lights flashing, flames licking twisted metal.

A faceless voice explained in a kind voice. "No, it wasn't his fault. Some idiot suddenly swerved into his lane. He must have jerked the wheel to avoid the col-

lision and lost control. Yes, he's still alive, but just barely. Yes, you can see him now."

"Philip, can you hear me? Philip, please don't die. I love you so. Please give me another chance. Oh, Philip, please don't die."

"PHILIP!"

The echoes of her scream filled the bedroom and Elizabeth Bannister jerked upright in her bed. Tears streamed down her face and her tumbled hair fell across her forehead, dotted with perspiration. She pushed her hair back with a shaking hand and began to take slow, deep breaths in an effort to calm her racing heart.

Would her nightmares never end? Philip had died over six months ago, but her dreams kept replaying their last conversation over and over, never deviating, never offering her an opportunity to change anything.

She had sat by Philip's bed for three days, waiting for him to regain consciousness, waiting to tell him he was wrong—he had to be wrong. She loved him and she truly wanted to marry him.

He'd never regained consciousness.

Elizabeth forced herself to get out of bed and go to the bathroom for a drink of water. She wondered when she would ever get a good night's sleep again.

All her friends had been so sympathetic and understanding about her grief. If they had only known how much she blamed herself. Maybe if he hadn't been upset with her, maybe if she could have explained—

Explained what? That she was merely a cardboard figure of a woman? That she didn't know how to reach out and involve another person in her life? That although she wanted to, she was afraid to get close to someone?

Philip had been right. He'd been extremely understanding and compassionate. But he had reached his limits.

No one knew he had ended their engagement the night of the accident. She hadn't needed to make any explanations. Her grief was certainly understandable.

She glanced into the mirror over the sink. Her cheekbones stood out too prominently in her face and her skin was too pale. She had never regained the weight she'd lost after Philip's death.

The alarm sitting next to her bed went off, cheerfully announcing it was time to begin her day. Elizabeth taught English literature at a small college in Westfield, New York. Her classes had been the only thing that had helped her keep her sanity.

Or had she kept it?

Sometimes she wondered. She knew Janine was worried about her. They had known each other since they'd been roommates in college. Janine had become the closest person in her life. She understood Elizabeth's background and her fear of attachment. Elizabeth remembered their telephone conversation from the previous weekend.

"Why don't you come on down here next weekend? It will do you good. You haven't been to Manhattan in over a year. I'll get tickets for a play. We'll go out for dinner. You need to make an effort to get out and see people again.''

Of course Janine was right, but Elizabeth had turned her down, out of habit more than anything else.

She had to break out of the endless whirling cage she seemed to occupy. She felt as though she were a small animal forever racing in circles, looking for a way out of the circular spin she was in. But how?

A sudden line of poetry sprang to her mind: *Had we but world enough, and time.* There was no more time for her to change things between Philip and her. His only legacy to her was tied up in his last words to her.

Had he been right? Was she incapable of loving anyone? She had seen so little love while growing up, how could she possibly recognize it? All Elizabeth knew was that with Philip she had felt warm and safe and comfortable. But there had never been a desire to become closer to him.

The grave's a fine and private place,
But none, I think, do there embrace.

Why did Marvell's poem keep coming back to her, with its wry message of how fleeting a lifetime can be?

With Philip in her life, Elizabeth had felt no need to explore her feelings. She had been content with her life and her career. Losing him had been one of the most traumatic things that had happened to her. It ranked right up there with the knowledge she'd slowly assimilated over the years that no one had ever really wanted her or loved her, not from the time she was born. Not until Philip.

And she had failed him. Learning to draw close to another person—to trust and rely on someone beside herself—was something that seemed foreign to Elizabeth. She had learned early in life to rely solely on herself. She was all she had. Even as a small child she had known that she must not ask anything of others. It was as though she had built an invisible force field around herself, and she remained inviolate and safe from the emotions of other people. Unfortunately her emotions had also been stopped from growing, as well.

The question now was, what did she intend to do about her life? She could continue the same way, refusing to let life touch her on any level, or she could reach out and begin to take part in the process of life again. The decision was hers to make, no one else's. Did she have the courage to take that first step into the unknown world of emotions and personal relationships?

She could try.

Elizabeth looked at the clock with a new determination. Was it too early to call Janine? She would take the chance. Picking up the phone by the bed, she punched in the numbers and waited as the phone rang repeatedly on the other end. Finally she heard a mumbled response.

"H'lo?"

"I was hoping you'd be awake by now," Elizabeth began.

"Oh, hi, Beth." Janine was the only person who had ever shortened Elizabeth's name. "Normally I would be, but we all worked late last night and I decided to sleep a little longer this morning. What's happening with you?"

"I was wondering if I could change my mind about your invitation for this weekend?"

"Of course you can! I'd be delighted to have you. How soon can you get here?"

"My classes are over at noon. Could you meet me at the station around four o'clock?"

"Certainly. And bring something festive and sexy to wear. I'm invited to a party tonight."

"Oh, don't let me ruin a date for you."

"It's not a date in that sense. I didn't want a date to this one. The host is Ryan Davidson, someone I met several months ago, who I definitely want to cultivate. He said I could bring a guest. You'll be perfect. Ryan throws the greatest parties because he knows the most fantastic people. It will give you a chance to greet the world."

Elizabeth smiled at her friend's enthusiasm. "I'm not at all sure I'm ready to greet the world just yet. But I've decided to at least open the door to it."

"That's a start, anyway. I'll see you at four. And I'll see what I can do about getting tickets for a show tomorrow night. We might as well make a grand celebration out of your visit."

Elizabeth felt her tension slip away. Janine would be good for her. Her uncomplicated view of life was just what Elizabeth needed at the moment.

* * *

"Would you stop fussing with that neckline, Beth? You look absolutely gorgeous. Just relax."

They waited at the bank of elevators in the lobby of Ryan Davidson's luxurious condominium building, watching the lights of the elevators signal the floor they passed.

"I shouldn't have let you convince me to wear something of yours, Janine. I don't feel at all like myself in this outfit."

"You look smashing. With your black hair and that flame-colored dress, you're going to be the hit of the evening."

"That's what I'm afraid of. What am I going to say when someone asks how much I charge?"

"Just because I refused to let you wear the dress you bought for your faculty soirees, that doesn't mean you now look like a professional call girl. Believe it or not, that dress is very conservative by New York standards."

"Why, because my navel is covered?"

Janine laughed and stepped into the elevator.

"Stop worrying. The only reason you keep tugging at the neckline is because the dress suggests you actually have a bosom to reveal. Let the unendowed eat their hearts out."

The party was well under way from the sounds of it when the door opened. Elizabeth had a sudden intense desire to turn around and run, but it was already too late. Janine had coaxed her into the foyer and was introducing her to a tall, smiling man with warm brown eyes and a mop of mahogany curls.

"Ryan, I would like you to meet my very good friend, Elizabeth Bannister. Beth, Ryan Davidson does something marvelously mysterious in international banking."

Ryan laughed. "Hardly mysterious, I'm afraid. Do you live here in New York, Elizabeth?"

"I live upstate. I'm visiting for the weekend."

"So glad you could come. Let me get the two of you a drink."

He turned and motioned for them to precede him across the open foyer and down the two steps into his massive living area. The room formed a circle. The outer wall was made of glass, except for a functional fireplace that added the rough texture of fieldstone to the elegance of glass and plush carpeting.

Elizabeth felt overwhelmed by the number of people, the bursts of conversation and laughter and the music that seemed to be competing with the voices. She would never become accustomed to this type of entertainment, but it certainly forced her out of her protective rut into modern-day life.

Her sweeping gaze paused momentarily and her eyes darted back to the fireplace and the man who stood in front of it. He looked relaxed and comfortable as he sipped from his drink and listened intently to the voluble conversation coming from a man several years his senior.

Why did she feel that she recognized him, when she was certain she'd never seen him before in her life? It wasn't so much his looks—because it was possible she'd seen a picture of him—but the essence of the man that seemed to reach out and draw her attention to him.

Ryan paused and introduced Janine and Elizabeth to a group of people and Elizabeth unobtrusively studied the man in front of the fireplace.

He wasn't particularly tall, but seemed beautifully proportioned. He had a classic, clean line that reminded her of another time, and she shook her head, feeling confused. Perhaps she had spent too much of her life reading poetry. She studied the way his hair, a mixture of brown gilded with blond highlights, framed his face. She couldn't tell the color of his eyes. A heavy fringe of dark lashes surrounded them. There were probably women who would kill for those long lashes, she thought with inner amusement.

His hands fascinated her; their slender length looked so capable, yet sensitive. He held his glass with unconscious grace while he gestured with the other one.

He must have felt her scrutiny, because he paused in what he was saying and glanced around, their gazes meeting with sudden impact. Elizabeth could feel the color flood her cheeks at being caught staring, and she tried to drop the gaze, but found herself unable to look away.

His eyes were gray—the soft gray of early morning before the new dawn has cleared away the mist. A magical feeling of inevitability washed over her. Elizabeth smiled.

Without taking his eyes off of her, the man slowly moved toward her, walking away from his companion as though he no longer existed.

What am I doing? she thought with sudden alarm. For a moment Elizabeth had forgotten. She was not in her small town any longer. This was not the place to smile at strangers. What had she been thinking of?

She forced her glance away and looked to Janine for assistance, but Janine was gone. She and Ryan had continued across the room, while she, stupidly, had stood there and stared at the stranger, who was inevitably coming closer.

"So there you are," were his first words when he paused in front of her. "I've been waiting for you."

His voice was low and it caused a rippling effect to spread through her. As he looked down at her, she was enveloped by his warmth.

"You have?" she heard herself respond, feeling at a loss.

"Yes. For years." He held out his hand to her and she glanced down helplessly. He was holding it toward her, not in the form of a handshake, but as a joining of the two of them. Feeling almost mesmerized, Elizabeth slowly placed her hand in his.

He smiled and his smile brought a flash of inherent beauty to his face, so that he seemed to glow with it. Suddenly Elizabeth felt as though she had been waiting for him to appear in her life for years and she recognized his greeting to be an acknowledgment of the

strong sense of familiarity that seemed to create a
bond between them. Deftly he guided her over to the
fireplace and to the man with whom he'd been speak-
ing.

"I'm sorry to have deserted you so suddenly, Henry.
I didn't want to take the chance of losing her in this
crowd," he explained with apparent sincerity. "Henry
is a writer," he offered.

"I'm Beth," she heard herself say to her own surprise, since she thought of herself as Elizabeth. This
man was having a very strange effect on her. "I'm an
inveterate reader," she said to Henry with a smile.
"Have I read any of your work, by any chance?"

Henry glanced at the two younger people standing
before him and smiled in delighted surprise. They
seemed so suited. He couldn't quite put his finger on
what it was. There were no visible characteristics that
were similar, but there was a sense of family—as
though they had grown up together, were in tune with
each other—that he found rather intriguing under the
circumstances.

"I write philosophy under the guise of science fiction, which I have found to be fulfilling as well as en-
joyable."

"Not to mention highly lucrative," his companion
added. He looked down at Elizabeth. "I'm very
pleased you made it tonight, Beth. I'm Dan, and I'm
in advertising." He continued to hold her hand,
strengthening the nonverbal bond forming between
them.

"Don't let him kid you, Beth," Henry chided gently. "Daniel Morgan is 'in' advertising the way Iacocca is 'in' automobiles. Dan has one of the most successful agencies on Madison Avenue. I've enjoyed watching his climb."

"Henry used to be one of my professors in college," Dan explained with a smile. "He tried his best to drum some sense into Ryan and me. The three of us used to sit around until all hours of the night in deep discussions about the meaning of life."

Henry nodded. "I think we all learned something from the experience. I quit teaching and started devoting myself to my writing full-time."

"Did you miss it?" Elizabeth asked with sudden interest. "The teaching, I mean?"

"At first. I missed the social interaction. Writing is a very lonely business. But I realized that writing was what I needed to be doing." He lifted his glass in a slight toast. "If you two will excuse me, I see someone over there I've been trying to talk to for some time." He knew they would barely notice his departure.

Dan and Elizabeth stood there in silence for a few moments and she searched for something to say. Bemused, she looked down at their clasped hands.

"What do you do when you aren't reading, Beth?"

She suddenly heard Philip's voice saying, "You live in another time with your English poets, refusing to face life," and for some reason she didn't want Dan to know who and what she was. For this one evening, she could be anything and anyone she wished and it wouldn't matter.

"If you promise not to mention it, I'll tell you. I spend most of my time visiting planets in this galaxy. Tonight was my turn to visit the planet Earth."

Her straight-faced explanation seemed to startle him, and she smiled. She could never remember having been so whimsical before. Everything in her life had always been governed by rules and regulations. There had never been time for fantasy and imagination.

His eyes seemed to dance with amusement. "Does Ryan know?"

She shook her head. "No one knows."

He moved closer to her and whispered. "Then your secret is safe with me."

They laughed and Elizabeth felt herself relaxing. This was going to be fun.

Daniel Morgan couldn't believe what his senses were telling him. This delightful young woman seemed to have bewitched him.

His first glimpse of her had shaken him more than he wanted to admit. She was like someone out of a dream he'd once had and had forgotten, until he glanced up and saw her watching him, waiting for him.

She was small, with satiny skin that looked like porcelain, warm but very pale. Her midnight-dark hair framed her face, accentuating the purity of her profile. But it was her eyes that fascinated him. They were so darkly blue they appeared almost black. Their almond shape gave her an exotic look that suggested she was not of this world.

He shook his head at his imaginings, unconsciously trying to clear it. The dress she wore made a brilliant contrast to her pale skin and dark hair, its vibrant red charmingly hugging her delicate curves, highlighting her small waist and curving breasts. Dan had a sudden urge to gather her in his arms to make certain she didn't suddenly disappear.

"May I get you a drink?"

She enjoyed the sound of his voice. Its deep quality seemed to wrap around her, hugging her with its warmth.

"Yes, please," she said, nodding.

"What would you like?"

She had no idea. Elizabeth rarely drank. "You choose."

When Dan returned, he handed her a fruit-punch drink that seemed innocuous enough and she gratefully sipped it, unaware of its potent content.

Dan found a small unoccupied sofa and motioned for her to sit down. "Are interplanetary travelers allowed to discuss their travels?" he inquired politely.

She took a quick sip of her drink to hide her smile. Demurely she explained, "Not really. We're here to study life on the planet. Would you mind telling me about yourself?" she asked politely. Pointing to her left ear and the small earring there, she added, "If you will speak directly into the microphone I won't have to bother taking notes."

Dan surprised himself by following her instructions. Casually he began to talk about himself, something he rarely did with anyone. Her obvious interest kept him talking, her questions spurring him on. A couple of times he refilled their drinks, unaware that she was not used to drinking.

The room glowed with a mystic light—or so it seemed to Elizabeth. She felt as though she had come to a costume party where no one had any idea who she was. She could do as she pleased, say the most outrageous things, and it was all right. Nothing seemed real.

"Why don't we go somewhere to eat? Would you like that?" Dan finally asked.

Elizabeth glanced around. If anything, the party had grown noisier and more crowded. She thought his suggestion was excellent.

"Let me tell Janine I'm leaving. I'll be right back."

Janine nodded absently when Elizabeth explained that she and Dan were going out for something to eat. "Okay. Glad you met someone nice. Ryan said Dan is a fantastic guy. I already checked him out for you. He's been married once, been divorced for years, doesn't date much, and Ryan was delighted to see him so engrossed in you." Janine kissed Elizabeth on the cheek. "Go and have fun. You've got a key. I'll see you back at the apartment."

Elizabeth floated through dinner and a couple of dances, but when she complained about the loud music Dan readily admitted the noise didn't help much with conversation.

She never remembered later how they ended up going back to his apartment, rather than his taking her to Janine's, but it seemed a very logical progression of events at the time.

"You live alone?" she asked, standing in the middle of a comfortably cluttered living area.

He grinned. "Can't you tell? I have someone who comes in once a week to straighten up the worst of it. Actually, I'm not here all that much."

"You work long hours, I can tell."

He motioned for her to sit down and then joined her on the couch. "Yes. But how can you tell?"

"Because you lead a lonely life."

Her comment startled him. Either she was astute at reading people or she was psychic. Either way, she was intriguing.

"I suppose I am, in a way. The agency has become my family. The wife I don't have, the children, the companion. I've enjoyed the struggle, but I guess I've never taken the time to do anything about widening my interests."

"Every life needs balance," she pointed out sagely.

"And is yours balanced?"

Of course not. I live a very one-dimensional life. I have no close friends, no family. I recognize your loneliness because it reflects mine.

"Of course mine is balanced," she replied. "All interplanetary beings lead balanced existences. Otherwise we would spin out of control instead of floating where we need to go."

He laughed, as she had meant him to. When he stopped laughing he kissed her.

Elizabeth wasn't prepared for his kiss. She had been around so few men in her life. Philip was the only man she had gotten to know well enough to allow his touch, and because he had recognized how untutored she was, his patient approaches had been very limited, she now acknowledged to herself.

She should not have enjoyed Dan's kiss. She should have pushed him away, explained that she had a problem, that she was afraid of people, of getting close, of physical intimacy.

But she didn't.

Elizabeth Bannister seemed to have retreated for a little while. Beth, the all-wise, all-knowing interplanetary being had taken her place. Beth relaxed and waited to experience the next few minutes with wonder.

As soon as Dan touched her he realized an astounding paradox. The beautiful, alluring, sensuous woman in his arms seemed to have very little experience. Her lips remained firmly closed, her hands rested in her lap. He felt no resistance coming from her, but very little response, either. He paused, pulling away slightly, and looked down at her. Her head rested on his shoulder and her eyes were closed. A slight smile hovered at the corners of her delectable mouth.

She seemed to be relaxed and enjoying their closeness, but she was making no effort to encourage him. Was it possible that she didn't know how? He began to wonder if her amusing story might have some merit, after all. Where else but outer space would he find a woman with so many loving attributes so seemingly untouched?

She opened her eyes slowly and stared up at him. When her gaze met his, she smiled, a slow, enticing smile that caused a tightening deep within him. He had never seen eyes like hers. They fascinated him, mesmerized him, made him forget who he was, who she was, and that he had only met her hours before.

"I want to make love to you," he said in a husky voice.

"Do you?" she replied in a sleepy-sounding tone.

"I know it's too soon."

"Of course," she wisely agreed.

"I guess I'd better get you home."

"Yes."

He continued to look at her curled up in the shelter of his arm. One more kiss wouldn't hurt. Then they would leave.

This time when he kissed her, he coaxed her to open her mouth. The kiss deepened and they both lost all sense of time, perspective, propriety and preservation.

Elizabeth felt as though she were truly a creature of the universe, floating in space, lost in the feelings that Dan evoked within her. She felt like a new person, full of freedom to explore and investigate these strange new sensations that Dan seemed to know were buried deep inside of her, waiting to be released.

Why did it feel as though she had always been a part of his life? Why did being in his arms seem so natural to her?

Their kiss became a prelude, a tentative joining of themselves to a new whole, a new being who had never before existed.

What was happening between them seemed natural and inevitable, as though they had been together many times before. Elizabeth felt totally at one with him.

Dan felt her tentative response to his kiss and his arms slowly tightened around her. He felt as though he were witnessing a cocoon as its occupant began to unfold and unfurl to become a living, quivering butterfly. Elizabeth's light touches on his face and shoulders seemed to loosen the restraints he'd placed on himself.

He was caught up in causing and watching her tentatively loving responses as he kissed her repeatedly, returning time and again to the soft sweetness of her mouth, as though drinking from the fountain of life.

She didn't stiffen when her dress slid from her shoulders and fell in a rich flow of color around her waist. His mouth and tongue began to love her with delicate touches, his hands softly caressing her. Instead she began to imitate his movements, removing his shirt and the clothing that seemed to prohibit her from enjoying the feel of his body against hers.

Later Elizabeth would wonder at what point she should have called a halt to what was happening. She would try to understand what had happened to her lifelong fears of inadequacy and her natural inhibitions.

But all she could even remember was the indescribable feeling of his gentle, tender kisses.

Chapter Two

Elizabeth woke up suddenly, her heart beating wildly, and for a moment she thought her recurrent nightmare had awoken her once more.

But this was worse. This wasn't a nightmare. It was reality.

The warm, hard body of the man who held her close caused her to remember what she had done. Her head swam, but she forced herself to try to think.

She was in Dan's apartment on Dan's couch with Dan's arms wrapped securely around her!

She had finally totally and completely lost her sanity.

Elizabeth lay there, trying to still her racing heart and her breathing, deathly afraid she would wake him up. What could she say to him? How could she possibly explain something she didn't understand herself?

She listened to his breathing, reassured by its strong, even rhythm. Could she get up without awakening him? She could only try.

By the time she was downstairs, thankfully crawling into a taxi, Elizabeth was shaking so badly she could scarcely stand. By New York standards it wasn't all that late. Probably Janine wouldn't think a thing about her coming home at this time. She might not even notice that Dan had not accompanied her.

What was she going to tell Janine? And how could she live with what she had done?

Only time would give her those answers.

"Did you have fun last night?" Janine asked over coffee the next morning.

Elizabeth refused to meet her eyes. "I suppose."

"You don't sound too enthusiastic. I'm surprised—the two of you seemed to find enough to talk about."

Elizabeth sipped carefully from her cup. "I know. At times I almost felt as though we were old friends, catching up on the years we'd missed in each other's lives." She set the cup down and forced herself to meet Janine's gaze calmly. "It was very strange."

"Is he going to call you again?"

"I doubt it."

"How can you be so sure? Did you argue or something?"

Or something. How can I explain what happened? I don't understand it myself.

"I think he was being polite, that's all." Besides which, he hadn't bothered to get her phone number.

Janine sighed, shaking her head. "What would you like to do today? We don't have to leave for the theater until seven."

Elizabeth forced herself to smile. "Something energetic that will get us out in the air."

"Just what I needed. A fresh-air fiend for a friend." She stood and placed her cup in the sink. "Well, don't just sit there. Let's get moving."

For the next two days Elizabeth forced herself to get into the spirit of the frivolous weekend, to push all her thoughts of either Philip or Dan out of her head. At least being with Dan had proved one thing. She wasn't frigid. She had enjoyed his touch. She'd felt safe and secure and had relaxed with him.

Perhaps now she would be able to let Philip rest in peace. She wasn't what he had needed in his life—she could better understand what he had tried to explain to her. What she had felt those few hours spent with Dan made a mockery of her relationship with Philip. She had failed him.

Facing that, and actually coming to terms with it, she could get on with her life, putting away her memories, of Dan as well as Philip.

The very thought of seeing Dan again made her shudder with embarrassment. At least she'd had enough sense not to tell him much about herself. There was no reason to think they would ever meet again.

Elizabeth made up her mind to treat the evening with Dan as a learning experience. It had certainly been that! She had come away from his apartment with the knowledge that she would never be the same again. Her entire perspective of herself and her life had made a sudden shift during those few short hours.

Although she recognized that she and Dan had shared something very special, Elizabeth knew she wasn't ready for a relationship with anyone. She needed to get in touch with herself, first.

Dan would never know the impact he'd made on her life. Unfortunately she was too embarrassed ever to risk contacting him to tell him.

She doubted very much if he'd care.

The hell of it was, he didn't even know her name.

Dan Morgan impatiently shoved his executive chair away from his desk and stood up. Sitting there thinking about her wasn't getting any work done.

So what else was new? Three months had passed since he'd met her. Three months since he'd spent an enchanted evening with a woman he'd never seen before. Or since.

Why couldn't he forget her?

Thrusting his hands into the pants pockets of his handsomely tailored suit, he wandered over to the window of his office and looked out at the traffic on Madison Avenue. He didn't see the traffic. Instead, smiling blue eyes stared back at him, their blue so clear he felt as though he could see down into the very center of her being. For three months that steady gaze had haunted him. Her eyes would suddenly appear to him as he fell asleep at night, or sometimes just as he began to wake in the morning. On a few occasions they had appeared in the middle of an advertising presentation to a client and he would be temporarily distracted, having to hastily remember where he was and force himself to continue.

Who was she? And why had she had such a profound effect on him?

He'd known many women in his thirty-seven years, but he'd never missed any of them as deeply as he now missed Beth. His marriage to Carol had ended almost eight years ago by mutual agreement. They had recognized that whatever had caused them to decide to face the world together got lost somewhere along the way to professional success. Their interests had diverged widely once they had launched their careers.

So why did he have such a sense of loss now, after spending one evening, a few short hours, with a woman he knew absolutely nothing about?

He had everything he wanted in life, didn't he? It was true that he had no family, but, then, he and Carol had congratulated themselves on having the wisdom not to bring a child or children into their busy world to be divided between single parents.

Had anyone asked him a few years ago if a family was an important element to him he would have shrugged the question off. Since meeting Beth, however, his thoughts had kept returning to a home and children, as though by her very arrival in his life, certain sparks of yearning for permanency had been ignited.

By any measuring stick, he'd be considered successful—but at the moment, none of his past triumphs seemed to matter.

He wandered back to his desk and sat down once again. For the past three months he'd become aware that something vital was missing in his life. Meeting Beth had brought the message home to him.

The question was—what was he going to do about it?

He knew he had rushed the relationship. He'd had three months to lament the fact that, given another chance, he would have handled the evening in a much different manner. But something important had happened between them. He was certain he hadn't imagined it. Why else would she have made love with him?

He still remembered his shock at discovering that she had never been with a man before, but by the time he'd become aware of the fact it had been too late to draw back, to apologize, or to question.

Dan Morgan wasn't in the habit of making love to a woman he'd just met, either, but she had no way of knowing that. He had thought he would explain later. At the time all he could do was dedicate himself to making her first experience as pleasurable and as satisfying as he knew how.

She had responded—he was certain of that. Her response had been hesitant, her inexperience obvious, but Dan had felt certain that she had wanted him, too.

Now he was no longer sure about anything.

When they had fallen asleep on his sofa, Dan would have sworn there was no way she could have moved without awakening him instantly. Yet she had disappeared from his life without a trace.

Dan leaned back in his office chair, disgusted with himself.

How had he managed to spend an evening with her and not find out her full name, where she lived, where she worked and how he could contact her again?

Was it possible he had dreamed their evening together?

He glanced at his wristwatch and decided to try once again to track her down by the only source he had. He picked up the phone and punched out a number.

"Ryan Davidson, please." He waited a moment, and when he heard his friend's voice on the phone he voiced his relief and frustration at finally making contact. "Damn it, Ryan, you have to be the hardest person to get in touch with I've ever known."

"Well, hello, Dan, it's great to hear from you, too," Ryan responded in a dry voice. "I take it you've missed me."

"Where have you been? I've been trying to reach you for three months."

"Earning my living. International banking does call for a certain amount of traveling," he drawled. "What's made me so popular with you these days?"

"I need to know a name."

"I had a feeling it wasn't my wit and charm that made you persist in your long search for me."

"I met someone at your party."

"Congratulations. Glad you decided to join the human race again. Who is she?"

"That's what I want you to tell me."

"Do we have a bad connection? You aren't making much sense."

"Her name is Beth and that's all I know."

"I don't remember any Beth at the party."

"Well, she was there—please take my word for it. She came with an attractive blonde that you seemed to know. Beth is a brunette . . . she wore a flame-red dress . . . looked like—"

"Oh, sure, I remember now. She came with Janine Shepard. I recall admiring your taste, now that you mention it."

"Fine. What's her name?"

"I don't remember. You know how it is when you're introduced to someone. I seem to remember the two of you sitting over in a corner, talking most of the evening." Ryan chuckled. "Are you telling me you forgot her name?"

"I never knew it. She introduced herself as 'Beth.' That's as far as we got with introductions."

"Well, I'm afraid I can't help you, Dan. I don't know any more than you do."

"What about Janine?"

"What about her?"

"Maybe she would give me her number, name, or something?"

"It wouldn't hurt to try. Of course Janine spends half her time on the West Coast, but maybe you can find her if you're that determined."

Dan's language turned the air blue, which only seemed to amuse his friend.

"I can't remember ever hearing you so over-wrought about a woman, Dan," Ryan offered. "She must have really gotten to you."

"Something like that."

"Well, I'll give you Janine's office number. Maybe someone there can help you locate her. Good luck, fella."

With a mixture of reluctance and relief, Elizabeth watched the students in her course on English Romantics file out of the room. The reluctance came because she no longer had anything scheduled for the rest of that Friday and she had an entire weekend free to try to come to grips with her life, something she didn't relish but could no longer postpone.

The relief came from knowing that despite everything that had happened to her recently, she had managed to remain professional enough not to display her turmoil to anyone around her.

She had managed to interest her students with the work of poets she had long admired: Blake, Words-worth, Byron, Shelley and Keats. For the time span of the class, Beth brought life into writings of different historical periods so that they tugged at the imagination of those who read them. In little more than six weeks of class, she had most of her students hooked, eagerly asking for more.

After locking the door to her classroom, Elizabeth left the English building, where she had taught for the past five years. The crisp October weather had changed the color of the leaves and lent a sharpness to the air.

She paused on the steps, breathing deeply, encouraged by the steady cycle of nature. Things changed yet ultimately stayed the same. She could count on the cycle of seasons to keep their time-proven progression—autumn, followed by winter, followed by spring.

Spring.

No matter where her thoughts might begin, they always ended up at the same place. There was no turning away, no pretending any more. She had to face herself, what she had done and how she was going to cope with the future.

Elizabeth tucked her chin into the upturned collar of her tweed coat and started across the grounds of the college. By following her normal routine in the small college town, she tried to instill in herself the courage to accept change without allowing it to completely destroy her peace of mind.

She needed to stop at the grocery store for Misty's cat food. There was also cleaning to pick up and a book newly released to buy at the bookstore.

Elizabeth had been alone most of her life. Sharing it with someone new would take some getting used to.

A slight stirring of excitement caught her unaware. No matter how often a sense of fear swept over her, a certain amount of anticipation continued to build.

Elizabeth Bannister crawled into her economy car, oblivious to the small smile on her face.

* * *

The morning sunlight brought Elizabeth a sense of well-being that had been missing in her life recently. She had been tired by seven o'clock the night before and had gone to bed early. She got tired much more easily these days, she realized.

There were a lot of changes going on inside her, she decided ruefully when she was unable to fasten the button on her jeans. *And it's going to get worse before it gets better,* she reminded herself.

So what if she seemed to have contracted a touch of pregnancy? She tried to be whimsical about a very serious situation. It wasn't as though she would be branded with a scarlet A on her forehead. She had always kept her private life to herself. When her condition became too obvious to ignore, she would come up with some reason why she had never told anyone about her marriage and eventual separation.

It was no one's business but her own.

What she had discovered in the deep soul-searching of the night before was that she very much wanted a child. In a matter of weeks the baby had become very real to her—someone to care about as well as care for.

Her own childhood had been so barren—placed in various foster homes, afraid to get attached to anyone because she knew they would never be permanent in her life. She had never felt she belonged anywhere.

Her baby would never have that feeling, she decided fiercely. He would know he was loved and wanted.

She stood in the kitchen, looking out the window at the back lawn, while she absently stroked Misty, a lilac-point Siamese who'd been entertaining her as well as keeping her company for almost two years. Together they watched the birds eating and the squirrels gathering nuts. No doubt Misty would love to run outside and make it clear they were there only because of her tolerance of their presence.

Elizabeth tried to picture a small child playing in the yard, and smiled. The cottage would make a good home for a child. They would have a comfortable life together; she knew they would.

The doorbell rang and she frowned slightly. She couldn't imagine who would be visiting her on a Saturday morning. She had no close neighbors and didn't know any of them very well, anyway. Janine was out of town and she always called first to make sure Elizabeth had nothing planned.

The bell rang again impatiently and she started for the door. More than likely it was a would-be magazine salesman who was eager to make as many calls as possible.

Elizabeth glanced into the hall mirror and grimaced. She had hastily put her hair up in a haphazard knot that already threatened to tumble down and her face was bare of makeup. Maybe it was close enough to Halloween to convince her visitor that she was a witch and to leave her alone.

She was smiling at the thought when she opened the door. Elizabeth froze. The sudden shock of seeing Dan Morgan on her doorstep took her breath away.

Dan had imagined several different reactions to his visit, but never had he pictured the expression of shock on Beth's face. For a moment he thought she was going to faint, but then she seemed to draw herself up to her full height, so that he could almost see the stiffening of her spine.

Here goes nothing, he thought with a mental shrug. "No one told me where interplanetary creatures rested on weekends, so I've had a bit of a problem tracking you down." He smiled, a tentative, almost vulnerable smile that seemed to spread warmth throughout Elizabeth's entire body. "So how have you been?"

He looked even better than she remembered him. The bulky hand-knit sweater he wore emphasized his tan and the light gray—almost silver—of his eyes. His smile caused the blood in her veins to rapidly heat.

When she first opened the door and saw him, Elizabeth thought she was going to faint. He was the last person she ever expected to see. Then the events that took place the last time they were together flashed in her mind and she could feel the color suddenly flooding her face. How could she possibly face this man again?

"Hello? Are you tuned into Earth language this morning?" he inquired politely. "May I come in?"

His quiet questions brought her out of her temporary paralysis and she nodded abruptly. "Of course. I'm sorry, you startled me." She stepped back, motioning him into the hall. As her gaze dropped, she realized with horror that she still wore the jeans that refused to button. The sweater she had grabbed hurriedly that morning had shrunk when she'd washed it. Her body was carefully outlined.

"Coffee is on the counter in the kitchen, if you'd like to go on back. Let me get into some presentable clothes," she said breathlessly.

His smile was gentle. "Don't change on my account. You look just fine." He took her hand and drew her down the hallway with him, pausing in the doorway of her sunny kitchen.

"It's like living outside, isn't it?" he asked. "You can almost hear the squirrels chattering and the birdsong is beautiful." He paused and looked down at her. "You're very fortunate."

"Yes. I've enjoyed living here."

"Have you been here long?" He seemed to be totally relaxed and at ease, as though they had only parted the day before.

"Uh, two years. I bought it two years ago." She poured the coffee and asked tentatively, "Have you eaten?"

He shook his head. "No. I left home early and didn't stop for anything but gas."

"You *drove* up here?"

"I enjoyed it. Autumn is my favorite time of the year."

"Why?"

"I'm not sure. It could be the way the air smells, the colors—"

"No, I mean why did you drive? Why are you here?"

His steady gaze met hers with calm deliberation. "To see you, of course."

To give herself a moment to come to grips with this unexpected arrival, Elizabeth began to search her refrigerator, pulling out the ingredients for an omelet. She tried to think of something to say, but her mind was blank.

"Janine said to be sure to tell you hello."

She glanced around at him. He had taken a seat in one of her captain's chairs, his long, muscled legs stretched out before him, his feet crossed at the ankles. He looked so natural sitting there, as though he were at home.

"When did you talk to Janine?"

"Yesterday. She's been out of town and I only managed to catch up with her yesterday afternoon." There was a certain amount of satisfaction in his tone that she didn't quite understand.

"I thought she was in Los Angeles."

"She is."

"And you called her out there?"

"Yes."

Once again Elizabeth was at a loss for words.

Dan decided he'd said enough for a while, so he sipped his coffee and enjoyed the peacefulness of Elizabeth's cheerful kitchen. Whenever he thought he could get away with it he would look at her, trying to drink in his fill of her like a man who had been in the desert for days without water. He was starved for the sight of her.

How strange, when he'd only been around her once. And yet he could have described how her face looked, how her skin felt, the shape of her eyebrows, the silkiness of her hair. It was almost as if she were a part of him.

She placed two plates of food on the table, poured more coffee, then sat down across from him and forced herself to eat. Elizabeth tried not to think about who he was and why he might be there. He had made a long trip and she had no reason to assume that his reason for looking her up was anything more than a sudden whim.

"Why did you disappear like that?" he asked finally, after paying her the compliment of eating everything on his plate. Either he had enjoyed her cooking or he hadn't eaten in a few days.

What could she say? "Does it really matter? That was several months ago."

"You don't have to tell me how long it's been—I know. And yes, it matters very much to me."

When she met his silver gaze she knew she owed him the dignity of the truth.

"I was embarrassed."

"About what?"

"About what had happened."

"You mean, because we made love?"

Why was it necessary to spell it out? She nodded her head. "Yes."

He reached over and touched her hand. "There was no reason to be embarrassed."

"I'm not used to going to parties and leaving with someone and . . ."

"I know. I was very much aware of that, believe me."

She could feel the color fill her face.

"You're still embarrassed," he said, a hint of disbelief in his voice.

"Yes."

With sudden decision he stood up and brought her to her feet. Circling his arms around her, he pulled her close to his body. "Nothing about our first meeting was normal, Beth—we both know that—but that doesn't mean you need to be embarrassed. We're way past that in our relationship."

She refused to meet his gaze. Instead she stared over his shoulder and watched a bluebird land on a branch near the window. "We don't have a relationship," she finally muttered.

Her attitude bewildered him, even though her friend had warned him. She was so different from the vivacious, smiling woman he had met in New York. What was wrong?

"Did I misread the situation?"

"What do you mean?"

"I thought what we shared that night was something very special. Was I wrong?"

"I didn't expect to ever see you again," she managed to hedge.

"Yes, I'll admit you did a very good job of being mysterious that night. But I thought that by the end of the evening you had begun to trust me. But I guess your disappearing act wasn't accidental. You had no intention of seeing me again."

She remained silent.

"Beth?"

Slowly her gaze left the window and she forced herself to look up at him. Was it possible she saw pain in his eyes?

"Yes?"

"I want to see you again. I'm not trying to create a complication in your life. I just want to be a part of it, whatever part you're willing to share." His hand slipped under her chin and his thumb rubbed across her cheek in a motion that Elizabeth felt was almost hypnotic. "Is that asking so much?"

"I don't date."

He waited, but she didn't elaborate.

"That's it?" he finally asked. "That's your explanation? Don't you ever make exceptions?"

"I have a full schedule of classes that keeps me busy and I—"

"So you're going to dismiss what happened between us, just like that? As though none of it matters?"

"I don't see any future in our trying to see each other, do you?"

"Yes, as a matter of fact, I do. I see as much of a future as either one of us cares to make of it."

She could feel the warmth of his body radiating through the sweater and tailored pants he wore. Unobtrusively she tried to step back from him, but he merely tightened the hold he had on her, bringing her even closer to him than before. Her breasts, slightly swollen and tender, pressed against his chest, and she could feel the bare stretch of her middle touching him where the sweater didn't quite meet to cover her un-buttoned jeans.

"It wouldn't work, Dan. There's no place in our lives for each other. We live too far apart to try to see each other except on the most casual basis."

His hands began to massage along the length of her spine. She felt so good to him and it had been so long since he'd held her in his arms. He had never wanted a woman as much as he wanted her. "I have never felt casual about you, not since the first time I saw you."

His lips sought the soft place on her neck where he particularly enjoyed touching, just under her ear, and he kissed her, keeping her close to him. Then he eased away from her slightly.

"So the answer is no," he finally said when she re-mained silent.

"I suppose, although I never heard a question."

"The question has to do with us, with our seeing more of each other, with deepening the relationship that we started a few months ago."

"Then the answer is definitely no."

He tightened his arms around her again and kissed her—a hard, punishing kiss. How could she say no to what they obviously shared? How could she pretend not to notice how well they went together, how well she fit him, how well her body—

He jerked back from her and glanced down. Her sweater had ridden up a little more, baring the slight beginning of a swell that disappeared behind the zipper of jeans that she was unable to fasten.

Dan could feel his heart begin to race at the thought of what such evidence could mean. Beth was slender, obviously not overweight, and yet—

Was it possible? But of course it was. Like some callow youth he had done nothing to protect her, and she—it had been her first time, of course she wouldn't have been prepared for what had happened.

He pulled away from her, searching her face for confirmation. Her cheeks were flushed and her eyes overly bright as she watched his expressive face register what he was thinking.

Dan dropped his hold on her and walked away, trying to come to grips with what he suspected and what it meant, if it were true.

She wasn't going to tell him. She was going to let him walk out of there without knowing. He felt a slow burning anger begin to build within him. If he hadn't spent the past several months playing detective he never would have found her, never would have learned about the consequences of their evening together.

Slowly he turned around and faced her from across the room. She stood there watching him warily, her arms protectively folded across her waist, effectively hiding the evidence.

With a deliberately level tone, Dan asked, "When is our baby due, Beth?"

Chapter Three

Hearing it spoken aloud made it seem so much more real, and Beth felt her heart leap at his question. She tried to think of something to say, but her mind was curiously blank.

"Don't try to deny it, because I won't believe you. You're at least three months pregnant and I know for a fact there wasn't anyone else before me."

"I'm not denying it," she said in a quiet voice.

"But you weren't going to let me in on your little secret, were you?"

His anger surprised her. "I don't intend to ask you for anything, if that's what you think."

"Am I supposed to feel grateful for that? Did it ever occur to you that I might want to know if I'm about to become a father?"

As a matter of fact, it hadn't occurred to her. From the moment she had learned for certain that she was pregnant, it had never entered her mind to try to contact him. How could she? His name was fairly common, and although she had been at his apartment, she knew she'd never be able to find it again if she tried.

She had never considered trying. It was as though the baby were a gift to her, to fill the loveless void in her life. Other women raised children on their own. It never occurred to her to think she couldn't. It didn't occur to her now.

"Are you saying you want to see my baby once it arrives?"

He walked over to her and stood there, watching her. "I'm saying that I want to do more than see it. I want to be part of its life, share in its care and feeding. I want to be a full-time father."

"But that's impossible. I mean, we don't even know each other. We live hundreds of miles apart. We—"

"We are going to become parents, Beth. All other considerations have to be set aside for the moment. We have shared in one of the greatest miracles life has to offer—we have created a life together. Neither one of us could have done it without the other. I believe I have just as much right as you do to be a part of our baby's life once it gets here."

Beth felt as though her knees were going to give way. Shakily she reached behind her and felt for the chair. She lowered herself slowly.

"I see," she finally managed to say.

"I doubt it. I'm not too impressed with your ability to see anything but your own wants and desires."

She glanced up at him, facing his anger. "There's no reason to be insulting."

"Beth, I haven't even begun to be insulting. I'm trying to make you look at this from a viewpoint other than your own. Do you think you're being fair to the baby, insisting on a single-parent relationship?"

"I never thought there was a choice."

"Well, think again. I am here to tell you that I insist on being dealt into this hand."

He walked over and poured what was left of the coffee into his cup.

After several moments of silence, Elizabeth asked, "What do you suggest we do?"

He forced himself not to show his relief that she had finally admitted he might have a say in the matter. She sounded uncertain, a feeling he could certainly identify with.

He moved over and sat down in the chair beside her and took her hand. "We'll work out something—you can depend on it."

"Have you ever wanted children?" For some reason she couldn't picture him with a family.

He laughed, a dry sound that echoed with irony. "I never felt I had a choice. All the women I know are too wrapped up in their careers to consider taking time out for a family."

"I understand their feelings. I've always been wrapped up in my career, too. That's one reason

Philip—'' With shock she realized what she had been about to say and she stopped abruptly.

Dan sat forward in his chair. "Who's Philip?"

"He was my fiancé," she said quietly.

"Was?"

"He was killed in an automobile accident last winter."

"Had you been engaged long?"

"Two years."

"And he had never made love to you?" he asked, his voice full of disbelief.

She bit her lower lip and shook her head.

"What sort of relationship was that?"

"A loving relationship. Philip loved me. And I loved him. We just weren't in a hurry and I—I needed time to—"

She couldn't say anything more.

After a few moments Dan sighed. "I'm sorry. I shouldn't have expected you to defend your decision. It just surprised me, that's all. You're such a warm and loving person that I—"

She shook her head, determined to stop him. "But that's the whole point. I'm not a warm and loving person. I never was. I've never let anyone get close to me, not even Philip. I kept postponing the marriage, kept insisting we wait, until—" her voice broke slightly "—it was too late."

Dan ran his hand through his hair, feeling her pain and wishing there were something he could say.

"I suppose your pregnancy came as quite a shock."

She attempted a smile. "You could say that."

"Life really has some strange twists, doesn't it?" He stood up and walked over to the counter, glancing with surprise at the cup of cooling coffee he had poured and forgotten. Looking at her, he said, "Why don't you put on something a little warmer and take a ride with me? We'll drive through the countryside, enjoy some fresh air, talk about what we can do about all this." He leaned on the counter. "It's not the sort of thing that can be ignored in hopes it will go away."

Maybe he was right. Nothing would be resolved by dwelling on the past. She nodded. "I'll be back in a few minutes."

Dan allowed himself a quick sigh of relief. He felt as though the building blocks of his life had been dumped out in front of him, all the pieces he'd put together so carefully lying in a pile, waiting to be sorted through and dealt with.

What still perplexed him was that he felt closer to Beth than to anyone he'd ever known, including his parents, Ryan or even Carol. He felt as though he could feel her pain, her uncertainty, her embarrassment, as though he were a part of her.

How could that be? They were strangers.

No. Never strangers. Not anymore.

He suddenly envisioned what it would be like to wake up every morning and find Beth beside him. Somehow he would have to convince her that their being together was a viable solution to their situation.

It would be the greatest campaign he'd ever launched, and the most important.

*   *   *

"You picked a beautiful day for a ride in the country," Elizabeth offered several hours later.

They had been driving in silence, each caught up in rather serious thoughts. She hoped to lighten the atmosphere somewhat.

Dan had been watching her unobtrusively as she quietly sat next to him in his small foreign car, trying to discover what it was about her that intrigued him so. She had a quiet stillness about her that he found very peaceful. Her serene expression touched him and he could almost see her sitting there holding a child. Their child. His heart lunged suddenly in his chest at the thought.

By what series of circumstances had they been brought together at that particular time in their lives? He certainly wasn't in the habit of picking up women and taking them home with him. In fact, he'd never done it before. That just wasn't his style. But it had seemed natural to share with Beth his retreat from the rest of the world.

And it had certainly been evident that she wasn't accustomed to such behavior. Suddenly he wanted to know more about her and Philip, and wondered how to ask.

"I'm glad you agreed to come with me," he finally replied. "I find the scenery much more pleasurable when I share it, don't you?"

She smiled. "That's hard to say. I rarely share anything in my life."

Hoping he sounded casual enough, Dan asked, "Did you and Philip enjoy getting out, enjoying the scenery?"

"Whenever he could get away. He had a law practice in Boston that took most of his time and energy."

So far, so good. She had answered the question as casually as he had asked. "How did you two meet, anyway?"

She smiled. "At college. He was the most persistent person I ever met. Eventually Janine, who was my roommate, felt sorry for him and joined him in insisting I spend some of my time on social activities."

"Why did you keep turning him down?"

"Oh, I don't know exactly. I was at school on a scholarship and I felt I needed to account for every minute of my time, just to prove myself worthy."

"What were your parents like?"

He felt her stiffen, and could have bitten his tongue for bringing up an uncomfortable subject.

"I don't know. I never knew them. I was raised in foster homes."

"So you don't have any relatives?"

"No."

"Do you stay in touch with any of the people you knew?"

"There was one—I called her Auntie Em—I wrote to once I left her home. She had fallen and broken her hip, so she couldn't look after me anymore, but she insisted we stay in touch. I think she was very proud of me. At least, I hope so." She glanced out the window. "She died my senior year of college."

They drove for a while in silence while Dan digested the information he'd been given. What it added up to was a person who had retreated inside herself, never allowing anyone to get close to her. For both their sakes, and for the sake of the baby, she needed to overcome her fear of relationships.

He hoped he could come up with the answer.

"Are you hungry?" he asked lightly.

"A little."

"Do you find yourself wanting to eat more these days?" he asked with a grin.

"Not really."

"Have you been to a doctor yet?"

"Yes."

"Why do I feel like I'm interviewing a reluctant guest on a talk show?"

"I'm not sure what you want me to say."

"Well, for starters, I'd like to know what the doctor said, if he thinks you're healthy, what suggestions he made for your diet and exercise. That's nothing major, I'm sure, but it's interesting to me, since I'm only going to be allowed to sit on the sidelines during this production."

"Oh. Well . . . he said I was healthy, a little thin for my height. He gave me some vitamins, told me to take care of myself and to come see him again in a month."

"Is that anything like take two aspirins and call me in the morning?"

"Similar. He forgot to warn me that if I didn't eat a large breakfast before taking the vitamins, they'd make me sick. But it didn't take long for me to figure that out.''

''What about morning sickness?''

''I don't have anything like that.''

''Then you're very fortunate. My sister was convinced she was going to die before she got past that stage.''

''I didn't know you had a sister.''

''You didn't? That's odd. I felt sure I told you every single, solitary thing about me the night we met. I must have talked for hours.''

''I enjoyed it. You're so different from the other people I know.''

''In what way?''

''Oh, more open somehow. More willing to share your thoughts and feelings. You aren't quite as regimented in your thinking as some of my fellow faculty members. I found you refreshing.''

''Not to mention forward.''

She wasn't sure how to respond to his last remark. ''Not forward exactly. It was just that I had never been in a situation like that before. Everything that happened seemed to be so natural that I never really knew when to call a halt to what was taking place.''

''I realized that later. I should have been in better control and normally I am, but that night seemed so different somehow. I can't really explain it.''

''I know. Neither can I. I didn't feel like me that night. I was someone else, someone witty and charming...alluring.''

"You still are, you know. Witty, charming and alluring."

"Actually, I'm rather shy."

They glanced at each other, holding the eye contact for a brief moment, and began to laugh.

Elizabeth recognized the absurdity of her situation. She experienced a tremendous relief to be able to share her feelings with someone else. Besides her doctor, no one else was aware of her pregnancy, even though she knew that sooner or later she would have to acknowledge it. Now that she felt herself relaxing, she discovered how much control she had kept over her feelings. She no longer felt a need to hide behind a facade of professionalism.

Dan stopped at a rustic inn for dinner. Elizabeth had not been out for dinner with anyone since Philip's death and she realized how much she had been punishing herself for what had happened to him, even though she knew she had had no control over the circumstances.

"Candlelight becomes you," Dan said with a smile.

Elizabeth self-consciously touched her forehead where curling wisps of satiny black hair fell from her topknot.

"I'm not really dressed for a place like this."

"Of course you are. You look beautiful."

He grinned as he watched her cheeks flush with soft color.

She couldn't help but think how much the soft lighting enhanced his finely chiseled features, the light reflecting in the silver-gray of his eyes. She wondered if her baby would have eyes like his and blinked in bewilderment at the unusual thought. There was every possibility that her child would look very much like the man seated across from her.

The dinner was leisurely and Dan kept the topics of conversation light because he knew what he had to say to Beth later might very well upset her. So he postponed that particular discussion until he took her home.

"Would you like some coffee?" she asked politely after inviting him inside.

"I don't think so. However, I would like to talk with you a few minutes before I start back."

She turned around from hanging up his jacket in surprise. "You're going back tonight?"

"Yes."

"That really isn't necessary, you know. I have a spare bedroom if you'd like to wait until morning."

"No. I have a presentation I need to work on tomorrow. I only need a few hours sleep and I'd rather get on the road tonight."

"Oh." She noticed that he seemed a little restless, and silently motioned him to her sofa. "Sit down."

He sat, watching her as she gracefully sank into the chair across from him. "I've been doing a lot of thinking today," he began.

Her eyes caught his attention once again, their serious expression causing him to pause and search for just the right way to say what he was thinking.

"I came here looking for someone who has haunted me for over three months."

Elizabeth didn't know what to say. She continued to watch him, a little wary of his next words, wondering why the relaxed companion of the day suddenly appeared so grim.

"You are already very special to me, Beth, or I wouldn't have taken the time and trouble to track you down. And I want... Oh, God, how do I say this? I want to have the right to be with you through the next few months, help with whatever I can. Do you understand that?"

"I appreciate your offer, but it isn't necessary."

He knew he wasn't getting across what he needed to say, but he had never been faced with such a situation before.

"I want to marry you, Beth," he finally blurted out.

He saw her flinch at his words and his heart sank.

"Marry me?" she repeated with disbelief.

"Well, it isn't all that strange, is it? Under the circumstances, I mean."

"But you don't even know me!"

"Is that what you're going to tell our child someday? 'Sorry, dear, but I couldn't marry your father. I didn't know him.'"

"Of course not. It's just that there's no need for us to marry."

"I believe that there is. And because I do, I think my wishes should count just as much as yours. I take it you don't want to marry me."

Elizabeth heard the hurt in his voice and she didn't know what to say or do to help minimize what he was feeling.

"Please don't take it personally."

"There's no other way to take it. It's a very personal matter. You happen to be carrying my child. How much more personal can we get?"

She shook her head, confused and upset. "I don't think I'm capable of marrying anyone," she finally admitted.

"There's nothing to it, actually. We can go before a justice of the peace, say a few words, sign a paper, and it's over."

"That's not what I mean. It isn't the ceremony—it's the living together afterward."

Dan allowed a sigh of relief to escape him. "Oh, is that all? Well, we can deal with that. I certainly am not going to insist on any husbandly rights, if that's your concern. Besides, you'll need to stay here and finish out whatever classes you have scheduled before the baby arrives. I'll have to stay in Manhattan...that's where I make my living, after all."

"Then what's the point of getting married?"

"So that our child will know that we are both willing to accept the responsibility of becoming parents. It's not as though we won't see each other. I can come up here. You can visit me over the holidays. I'm hoping you'll consider coming to New York to have the baby, so I can be with you."

He watched the expressions on her face, trying to will her to see how important their marriage was.

"Would it have to be permanent?" she asked thoughtfully, and once again his heart sank. She wasn't even going to consider making it a true marriage.

Dan had never thought so quickly in his life before. Nothing that had happened to him had been this important and he didn't want to blow the whole thing by some hasty remark.

"I will leave that decision up to you, Beth. Why don't you see how you feel after the baby comes? If you find marriage too restrictive and want your freedom, I won't fight you."

"What about the baby?"

"I think we both care enough about the baby to decide, when the time comes, to do the best thing for all three of us. Don't you?"

How could she know that? How could anyone know how another person might behave? As far as she knew, the minute she said her vows he could become some raving maniac, forcing her to his will.

She almost giggled at the absurd thought. Dan Morgan was the least likely person she knew to become a maniac.

"All right."

That was it? All right? he thought. He had just managed to convince her to marry him and she was sitting there quietly, watching him, as though they had agreed on the next political candidate to run for governor.

"Fine." He stood up, determined to leave before he said something that might blow the whole situation. He went over to the hall closet and retrieved his jacket. "I'll give you a call sometime next week so we can make the final arrangements as to when and where, if that's okay.''

She nodded. ''Okay.'' She had stood when he did and walked over to him.

Carefully he slipped his arms around her waist. ''Thank you, Beth. I promise that you won't be sorry you trusted me. I won't abuse that trust.''

Her smile was a little wobbly, but her gaze was steady as it met his. Elizabeth had already discovered that Dan enjoyed physical contact. She recognized that he wasn't even aware of how often he ran his finger along her cheek, took her hand in his, or as now, placed his hands around her waist.

He didn't mean anything by it, she knew. She would just have to get used to it. Actually, Elizabeth had discovered earlier that day that she rather enjoyed being close to him, which was strange. She'd always resented other people who made a habit of trying to touch her.

Dan Morgan was different somehow.

Forcing himself not to pull her into an embrace, Dan leaned over and contented himself with a soft kiss. Her mouth relaxed under his, surprising him. Their one night together seemed to have taught her something about how to share a kiss.

Almost imperceptibly, he drew her closer, savoring the lack of resistance as she allowed him access to her warm mouth. Ever mindful of not frightening her, he deepened the kiss, delicately touching her with his tongue, exploring softly as though reacquainting himself with her once more.

Elizabeth recognized the melting sensation within her that had caused her to lose all her inhibitions the first time she'd met him, and slowly stiffened.

Dan immediately slackened his hold, although there was no way he could disguise the effect she had on him.

His harsh breathing sounded loud against her ear as he held her to him, stroking her back with a trembling hand.

"I'm sorry. I didn't mean to come on so strong."

She smiled into his shoulder. "That's all right. All this is just a little confusing to me right now."

"I know, and I don't want to add to the confusion." He dropped his hands and stepped back. Giving her a crooked smile, he said, "Besides, I need to get moving." He reached behind him and opened the door. "I'll call you in a few days."

"Do you have my number?"

He grinned. "Yes. Janine was very thorough."

"Why didn't you call before you drove up?"

He didn't want to admit how afraid he'd been that she would refuse to see him. He hadn't wanted to give her a choice.

"Oh, I needed to get away for a while. Even if you hadn't been home I would have enjoyed the trip."

"Take care driving back."

"You can count on it. I'm not going to take any chances that I won't be around." His grin was contagious and she responded with a smile that caused a lump to form in his throat.

"Bye, Beth."

"Bye, Dan." She had never corrected him about her name. Actually, she rather liked his calling her by that name. It brought him closer somehow.

Dan strode over to his car and got in, determined to get away from there before he allowed her to see what he was really feeling.

She had agreed to marry him. He had to keep that thought in mind and not let the stunning revelation he'd experienced when he'd held her in his arms to disrupt his thinking. He would need to make plans, discuss options and try to treat the coming marriage as though it were no more than a business merger.

Under no circumstances must he allow Beth to realize that he had fallen in love with her. If he did, he knew he'd never have a chance of winning her on a permanent basis.

And win her he was determined to do.

Chapter Four

November 2 was a cold, blustery day in New York City. Dan met Elizabeth's train and she felt a moment of wonder that the man standing there, so attractive and radiating a quiet self-confidence, would be her husband in a few short hours.

She was aware of the moment he first spotted her—his face lit up in a smile that almost took her breath away. If he had any doubts about what they were about to do, he certainly hid them well. He was beside her in a few strides, picking her up and swinging her around with an exuberance that caught her unaware.

"I didn't think you were ever going to get here!"

She glanced at her watch in surprise.

"Oh, the train was on time. It's just that I've been counting the hours."

He draped his arm across her shoulder and hurried her to the exit of the station. "Are you hungry?"

She started laughing.

"What's wrong?" he demanded.

"Nothing's wrong. I just feel as though I've been whisked off the train by a whirlwind and I'm not sure what I'm supposed to do or say."

He grinned sheepishly. "Sorry." He pulled her closer to him. "Is it all right to be excited on my wedding day?"

Since she had been unable to sleep at all the night before and her heart had been indulging in aerobic exercises all morning, Elizabeth didn't feel she had any room to criticize. She smiled up at him. "I'd much prefer you to be excited than upset by it," she admitted shyly.

"I hope it's all right with you . . . I asked Ryan and Janine to stand up with us."

Elizabeth stopped walking abruptly. "You told them about us?" she asked, her eyes wide with apprehension.

Oops, you really blew it this time, Dan admitted to himself. He guided her into a waiting taxi before answering.

"I didn't realize you intended our marriage to be a secret."

"I didn't. I mean, I don't. But I suppose I thought we'd just go do it and not mention it to anyone."

"Why?"

"Because of all the questions and everything."

"Beth," he explained in a carefully neutral tone, "there were no questions other than why we didn't let anyone know sooner. As far as people are concerned, what we're doing isn't unusual."

"Janine knows better."

She knew her friend very well, Dan decided. He'd spent a rough few minutes on the phone when he called and told Janine of his plans. Somehow his sincerity must have come across, because she eventually believed he knew what he was doing. She wasn't as sure about Elizabeth.

"She sounded very pleased for us," he said cautiously, leaving out ninety percent of their conversation regarding the marriage.

"You told her about the baby," she stated in a flat tone.

"No."

"You didn't? Then what reason did you give for our getting married?"

"The oldest reason in the world. We fell in love and wanted to spend the rest of our lives together."

"Oh, Janine would never believe that."

"She did." *Eventually,* he added silently.

"I should have called her. Was she upset that I hadn't told her?"

"More surprised than upset, I'd guess. I explained that you had asked me to notify her and she accepted that. Frankly, it never occurred to me that you wouldn't want her to know. She was pleased her schedule permitted her to be with us today."

Elizabeth heard the bewilderment in his voice and realized that her attitude was ridiculous. Unaware that she did so, she impulsively reached over and took his hand, squeezing it lightly. "I'm glad she's going to be there. The news just caught me by surprise. Thank you for thinking of her."

Dan stared down at her hand, at the delicate shape of it, resting so trustingly in his. He felt as though that same hand had squeezed his heart, and for a moment he couldn't think of anything but the fact that for whatever the reason, this woman had agreed to marry him. He was more aware of the trust implied in that gesture than ever before, since Janine had explained more of Beth's background to him, as well as her relationship with Philip.

Poor Philip. He must have really loved her and she had seen him as a brother, although Beth didn't seem to realize that. Philip had wanted more from her than she had been willing to give. Was he, Dan, making the same mistake by hoping that with time and patience their marriage could become a complete sharing of themselves with each other? Only time would tell, and Dan had more than enough time to spare.

Janine and Ryan were waiting for them at the civil office where the ceremony was performed.

Later Elizabeth could barely remember what had taken place, it had happened so fast. All she knew was that after a very short period of time they were all leaving and she was wearing a golden band decorated with several diamonds worked into an intricate design.

"I didn't get you a ring," she said quietly while Janine was listening to something Ryan was saying.

"You still can, you know," he said with a smile.

"Would you want to wear one?"

"If you chose it for me, yes, I would," he admitted.

"I would like to propose a toast," Ryan said later over dinner. "To Dan and Beth, a pair who seem to belong together. May your forevers continue in peace and joy."

They all laughed and sipped the champagne that Ryan had ordered for them.

"You know, that's true," Janine admitted. "I noticed the first night they met how suited they seemed to each other."

Dan glanced down at Elizabeth, who wrinkled her nose at him. He laughed, recognizing her self-consciousness.

"Well, as you can see, it didn't take me long to make sure Beth was convinced we belonged together." He reached under the table and gently squeezed her hand.

They were all going on as though the marriage were perfectly normal, and Elizabeth wondered what Ryan and Janine were going to say when they discovered she was going to have a baby in a little more than five months' time. Would they feel as though they'd been tricked into believing the marriage was a love match?

She had no idea and she wasn't ready to face their reactions just now. She silently blessed Dan for his instinctive understanding of her feelings.

Elizabeth knew that Dan would never intentionally cause her distress. It was a warm, comfortable feeling and she felt a surge of freedom at the thought. He might not love her, but he respected her and was willing to give her the space she needed.

Dan Morgan was a very unusual man and she was beginning to realize how fortunate she was...in many ways.

"There's one thing I haven't mentioned," Dan began as he let her into his apartment later that evening.

He sounded so worried she felt an immediate need to soothe him. Instead she waited for him to continue.

"I only have one bedroom here and I was hoping you wouldn't feel it too restrictive if we shared it whenever you were in town."

Step number two was just about to be launched. If the first step was getting her to agree to marriage, the next step was to get her accustomed to the casual intimacy of marriage.

"I have an oversize bed, so I'm sure you won't feel crowded. Actually, three or four people could rest comfortably in it." He led her across the living room and flipped on the light in the bedroom to show her what he meant. The room was decorated in shades of warm browns and tans. A very masculine room. And the bed was indeed large.

Elizabeth tried her best to overcome the faint panic she felt at sharing a bedroom with him. Of course she knew he wouldn't attack her. He'd made it very clear that she had nothing to fear from him in that regard. So what was wrong with sharing the room with him?

She already knew him well enough to know that he wouldn't allow her to sleep on the sofa and she felt it unfair to expect him to give up his bed for her.

Walking over and glancing into the bathroom, she kept her face turned away from him when she said, "I'm sure there will be room enough for both of us." Then she turned around. "I doubt that I will be here all that much, really."

Oh, yes you will, if I have my way, he silently disputed.

"Great. You're welcome to the bathroom first, if you'd like."

She really was tired. The busy day—combined with no sleep the night before and the champagne at dinner—had almost caused her to fall asleep on the way to Dan's apartment.

"Thank you. If you don't mind, I think I will get ready for bed. I'm a little tired."

He walked over and cupped her face in his hands. "You may be tired, but you look radiant. You made a beautiful bride, Mrs. Morgan."

She could feel that melting sensation once again, and this time he hadn't even kissed her. Elizabeth couldn't understand the effect he had on her. She went up on tiptoe and kissed him lightly on the lips.

"Thank you for today. You made it very special."

He could have cheered at her totally natural response to his touch. Instead he kept his tone matter-of-fact. "I wanted it to be special for you because you're very special to me."

He immediately saw the flash of apprehension in her eyes and hastened to find a suitable explanation for his remark. "You're the mother of my unborn child and deserve the best I have to offer."

He could feel her relax and realized how close he'd come to undoing everything he had managed to accomplish so far.

"I almost forgot about the baby today, what with all the excitement. I suppose we should have told Janine and Ryan," she suggested reluctantly.

"We'll tell them soon enough. Chances are we won't be seeing very much of them, not with their travel schedules. It's a wonder they ever manage to be in town at the same time."

"Do you realize that your college roommate and my college roommate introduced us to each other?" she asked, her eyes dancing with amusement.

"Which just goes to prove that higher education is never wasted. Do you suppose they're going to demand a commission or something?"

She laughed, and he realized how often he tried to amuse her so he could hear her clear, tinkling laughter.

"Did you tell your students you were getting married?'

"No. I've never given details of my personal life to my students. As far as any of them know, I've been married for years."

Dan had a glimpse into the lonely life Beth had built for herself and vowed that he was going to do everything in his power to show her the rewards of sharing with others.

He patted her familiarly on her bottom and said "Go get your shower, woman. I'm about ready for bed myself."

Startled by the intimate gesture, Elizabeth glanced up and saw the watching amusement in his eyes. *I refuse to get rattled by our new relationship. But it isn't fair. He's already accustomed to being married. This is all very new to me.*

She disappeared into the bathroom, while Dan walked over and turned back the covers of the brand new bed he'd had delivered the day before.

Elizabeth had hoped she would be asleep by the time Dan came out of the bathroom. No such luck. When he opened the bathroom door she almost leaped straight up.

Stop being ridiculous. You're a grown woman, for heaven's sake. Your attitude is absurd. Dan Morgan knows you better than any other man. There is nothing to be afraid of.

Her little pep talk helped immensely and Elizabeth managed to relax somewhat, until she felt his weight on the bed and realized he was now lying somewhere nearby. She could feel herself tensing and deliberately began some deep-breathing exercises she had learned in an effort to relax several months ago.

"Good night, Beth," he said from the darkness.

"Good night."

"Are you warm enough?"

She felt that her racing blood had warmed her body to the point where she was probably feverish. "Yes. I'm fine."

She waited, but he didn't say anything more. She felt the bed move and decided he must have turned over. Great idea. She gingerly shifted to her side so that her back was to him.

Turning over was the last thing she remembered.

Sometime during the night the warmth of two bodies must have proved to be irresistible. That was the only explanation Dan could think of when he awakened sometime in the early dawn to find Beth curled up in his arms.

Her head was on his shoulder, her hand rested on his chest and her knee was nestled rather intimately between his thighs.

His body had already reacted to her provocative position and he gingerly began to move away, hoping she wouldn't wake up and think he had coaxed her into that position.

Nothing could have been farther from the truth. Dan had lain awake for hours, all too aware of their proximity and knowing he had no intention of doing anything about it.

He still couldn't believe he'd managed to convince her to sleep with him their first night together. He was not going to ruin that strategic gain by letting her discover how much he wanted to make love to her. And if she woke up now, there was no way she would not know.

She sighed when he tried to remove his arm from under her head and he froze. When she didn't stir, he began once again to move his arm, slowly, ever so slowly, until it was free. Next was her hand and knee.

Inching away from her, he finally managed to free himself, and crawled over to the edge of the bed, when what he wanted to do most in the world was pull her closer and enjoy all the marvelous ways two people could enjoy each other. The need to reexperience what they had once shared had tortured him for months, but he reminded himself to be patient. Time was on his side, if he managed the situation correctly.

She was definitely worth the wait.

Elizabeth dreamed once again, but this time it wasn't Philip who stood there telling her he wanted out of their relationship. It was Dan's voice that told her he was tired of waiting, tired of trying to make love to a two-dimensional person who had no feelings or emotions.

She called his name, but he didn't answer. He walked away disappearing into the mist, and she awoke with a sudden jerk.

Faint daylight lit the room. Her heart was pounding and she couldn't remember where she was. Then the events of the day before fell into place and she realized she was at Dan's apartment.

He was practically hanging on to the edge of the bed because she was sprawled across the middle. How embarrassing. Hastily wriggling back to her own side, she tried to come to grips with her dream.

She had never seen Dan as he had appeared in her dream and Elizabeth faced the fact that she would never want to. She had to acknowledge that she cared too much for him to want to see that look of contempt that her dream state had transposed from Philip's face to Dan's.

She could never blame Philip. She hadn't shown him affection. Her love for him had been too internalized, but now she had a chance to show Dan that she appreciated him. The question was how.

He had never given her any reason to believe that he wanted more from the relationship than what they had originally agreed upon. She would have to be careful not to disgust him with open displays of affection.

She didn't know much about giving affection, but there was no time like the present to begin to learn. With that resolve, she relaxed and fell asleep once more.

Elizabeth awakened sometime later to an empty room, filled with sunshine. She had just thrown the covers back and stood up, when Dan appeared in the doorway.

"Good morning."

Dan hadn't meant to startle her, but he didn't want her to think she was married to a Peeping Tom, either, so he had spoken as soon as he realized she was awake.

Elizabeth glanced over her shoulder and hastily grabbed the robe she'd left out the night before.

"Good morning."

"Coffee's made and breakfast is started."

She smiled. "What service."

"You provided the same for me when I was visiting you."

"That's true."

"Anyway, I'm used to getting up early and saw no reason to disturb you." He wondered if she was aware of their cuddling position the night before. "Did you sleep all right?"

She flushed, remembering how much room she'd taken up. "Oh, yes, thank you. How about you?"

Other than facing a cold shower at six in the morning, he'd done very well. "I was fine," he managed to say. He walked over to her. "I enjoyed waking up and finding you in my bed."

She tried to laugh, but it sounded a little shaky. "That sounds a little different than it really was."

"I'm still very pleased to have you here. I hope you'll be comfortable."

"Oh, yes. I'm sure I will be." Remembering her early-morning resolve, she shyly slid her hands around his waist and hugged him. "You're a very genial host."

Dan felt as though someone had suddenly knocked the breath out of him. Her move had caught him totally off guard.

He didn't know what to do with his hands. Left to their own devices, he was certain they would naturally fall and cup her delectable derriere. Concentrating on keeping them above her waist, he placed his hands lightly on her back.

When she lifted her face and trustingly closed her eyes he almost groaned. Obviously his willpower was going to be tested in the coming months. The question was, could he deal with the temptation without succumbing?

Dan attempted a light kiss on her rosy mouth only to discover that she was prepared to participate in a long, leisurely kiss that effectively wiped out all his plans for a safe distance between them.

Elizabeth enjoyed Dan's touch. She tightened her hold, running her hands along his strong muscular back, enjoying the feel of his bare skin against the sensitive pads of her fingers. Although he wore a sweater, she had quickly run her hands beneath it in order to touch him.

The thin gown and matching robe she wore proved to be no protection from Dan's restless hands. The kiss deepened and he felt her breasts pressing against his chest.

She felt so good in his arms. For a moment he forgot his plan. Instead all he remembered was that he held his wife in his arms and that he loved her very much.

He had picked her up and placed her on the bed before he realized what he was doing. Forcing himself to loosen his hold, he sat down beside her, releasing her gently.

"You go to my head, did you know that?" he whispered on a ragged breath.

"You seem to affect me the same way," she admitted, embarrassed to meet his gaze.

"I think maybe we should go have some coffee and consider getting some fresh air, don't you?"

She wondered why she felt so disappointed, when she had never had any intention of having an intimate relationship with him. She wasn't ready for that. Or was she?

Elizabeth couldn't understand what was happening to her. How could she have changed so much from the person who had been engaged to Philip? How could she have felt so strongly for Dan, a complete stranger, the first time she met him? Why did she feel that she wanted more than anything else to experience his lovemaking again?

She sat up, pushing her tumbled hair away from her face. "I think maybe you're right."

He grinned, rubbing her cheek lightly with his thumb. "I was afraid you'd see it my way."

She laughed, suddenly free from her embarrassment and chagrin at the unfamiliar sensations he provoked whenever he touched her.

Elizabeth had never known anyone like Daniel Morgan. She was almost convinced he was one of a kind.

She discovered that she wanted to be the kind of person he deserved—a warm, loving woman who could give back to him as much as he gave.

She would have to give that some thought. Sharing yourself with someone else was never taught in school. Elizabeth wasn't sure how she could study up on it.

But she knew she was determined to learn.

Chapter Five

The day before Thanksgiving arrived with blowing snow and traveler's advisories not to travel. A sudden gust of wind caused the limb of a tree to brush against the window, and Elizabeth woke up with a start.

She sat up in her bed and stared out the window in consternation. The snow that had started the evening before continued to fall. With a feeling of dismay, Elizabeth reluctantly settled back into bed again.

He would never be able to make it up there today. Glancing at the clock on the bedside table, she decided she might as well get up. The alarm would go off in another half-hour, anyway.

She shoved off her covers and felt around for her fuzzy house slippers, feeling the draft of cool air on her ankles.

Tugging on her warm, old housecoat, Elizabeth padded over to the bathroom, trying to fight her disappointment.

She hadn't seen him since their wedding three weeks earlier and had been counting the days until Thanksgiving. When Dan called last night, his plans were to leave Manhattan no later than three o'clock, which meant he'd arrive at her house that evening.

Neither of them had expected the snow to hang around and become a full-fledged winter storm.

Changes had taken place during the past three weeks. Physically her body had taken on a spurt of growth that had forced her to go shopping earlier than she'd planned to find some comfortable clothes. It was as though the baby had suddenly decided to get serious about the idea of growing and becoming part of the world.

She methodically soaped her body and glanced down at her stomach with a slight smile. No one looking at her could possibly make a mistake about her condition now.

Not that she had any trouble seeing her toes, but given the fact that she seemed to have doubled in size in the past few weeks, she had a sneaky hunch her toes might disappear from view any day now.

She wondered what Dan would think when he saw her. If he saw her, she mentally corrected herself.

There had been some emotional changes, as well. His nightly phone calls had made a considerable difference in her life.

Elizabeth absently reached for the water control and turned it off, then stepped out of the shower.

Only her daily routine had stayed the same. She still taught her classes, came home and graded papers, prepared for classes and in her spare time read and watched a little television.

Dan's phone calls had become a focal point in her life. They usually came between nine and ten o'clock each night.

She smiled at some of the nonsensical conversations they'd had.

"Good evening," Dan had said one night last week, "I'm trying to get in touch with an interplanetary traveler and was told she could be reached at this number."

He'd sounded very professional and serious.

"Perhaps I could help you," she replied, trying to hide her amusement.

"Oh, I sincerely hope so," came his relieved reply. "I understand that traveling between planets can become quite an ordeal, particularly when it comes to finding your favorite foods. Have you noticed any problem in that area?"

"Not really. You'd be surprised how innovative McDonald's and Burger King have been in expanding their franchises."

"Why, I had no idea! I'm sure you find it a relief. But does a Whopper really taste the same on Venus?"

"Close enough. Their mustard has a strange consistency, though. But that's just one of the hazards of traveling we learn to accept."

"I've been meaning to ask—have you noticed a tendency lately to crave certain unusual foods?"

"Well, yes, now that you mention it," she admitted thoughtfully.

"I knew it. I had a strong hunch that you were feeling deprived stuck up there with nothing but students and faculty to look after your needs."

Elizabeth could almost see his eyes sparkling with amusement when he paused.

"What are you craving?"

"Pretzels."

"Pretzels! Those aren't rare and exotic."

"I never said they were."

"But I expected you to want something that was hard to find, like strawberries, or maybe watermelon."

"Sorry. I just like to munch on pretzels. It's probably the salt or something."

"I don't suppose you have any trouble finding them at the local market, huh."

"Not at all. In fact, I'm enjoying some now. Care to join me?"

"Very much. But not to help you eat pretzels." His voice dropped slightly. "I miss you, Mrs. Morgan."

And she missed him, too, which seemed very strange to her. She didn't even know him, and had only been around him a few times. Perhaps it was her pregnancy that was affecting her usually sensible attitudes.

"Is this where I'm supposed to recommend two aspirin, et cetera?" she asked with interest.

He laughed. "I'm afraid that won't cure what ails me. So how have you been?"

"Since last night when I talked to you?" she asked, her amusement obvious. "Fine."

"Are you making fun of me?"

"Not in the least. The phone company must love you."

His voice sounded serious. "Would you prefer that I not call so often?"

"I enjoy hearing from you, Dan." She was surprised to discover how true that was.

"I think about you often, you know. I seem to have developed the habit and can't seem to break it."

"How did your presentation go today?"

"Extremely well. I seemed to be in rare form. Got the account, which means I'm going to have to hire some more help. I seem to be expanding faster than I dreamed possible."

"I'm happy for you."

"How about you? Are you expanding on schedule?"

"Yes, as a matter of fact, I am."

"When do you go to the doctor again?"

"The day after Thanksgiving."

"Great. I'll be there to go with you."

"Are you sure you want to?"

"Absolutely."

"If you weren't planning to come up here, how would you be spending your holidays?"

"Oh, I don't know. I might have gone out of town, visited some friends in Virginia. Or I might have stayed here and worked up some ideas for an upcoming campaign. Why?"

"I just wondered. You seem to have adjusted very well to not having a family."

"My sister and I are still close, if that's what you mean, but she's busy with her family in California."

"I was thinking about your parents."

"They've been gone a long time, Beth, as I explained the night we met."

"I remember. You seemed so well adjusted about it all."

"That's because I don't believe in living in the past. They had a happy life together, and Mom didn't outlive Dad by more than a few months. They gave us their love and expected us to pass it on to our families."

"You were very lucky."

"Yes, because now I have a family to share all of that love with."

"I wish I had known my parents." She had finally put a secret wish into words for him.

"Once you get involved with our baby you'll probably discover that your parents gave you what was most important—your life and your ability to make whatever you want out of it."

"I suppose. At least, I'm working on that attitude these days."

"Glad to hear it. There's nothing more futile than looking back and wondering 'what if,' since there's not much we can do about our past."

"As a matter of fact," she said thoughtfully, "my daily life seems to be picking up considerably."

"How's that?"

"Oh, my students are becoming inquisitive. Someone noticed the wedding band, another noticed my new style of clothes, and they've actually come up and casually questioned me."

"And how did you handle their questions?"

"Differently than I had imagined I would. They seemed truly interested in me the person, rather than as their professor. It surprised me. I explained that we had what was considered, I suppose, a modern marriage, and that we commuted to be together."

"And what was their response?"

"Even more interest, since many of them are trying to reconcile career possibilities with strong ties they are currently forming. I was amused that they treated me as though I were an expert in those areas."

"Did you enjoy yourself?"

"Yes, I really did. I ended up having coffee with a couple of the women—one who had been married a couple of years, the other still contemplating what would be the right choice for her. I rather enjoyed being part of the group, sharing my thoughts and feelings about society and the way it functions."

"So there's a good possibility I might call some evening and find that you're not at home," he suggested.

Elizabeth heard the pleasure in his voice and wondered about it. "Oh, I doubt it, at least not during the week. I still need my sleep."

"Which reminds me. It's past your bedtime. Take care of yourself . . . I'll call you tomorrow night."

"You take care, too. Thank you for calling."

She'd hung up smiling. It was fun to have someone to share her day with. And it gave her something to look forward to, waiting to hear from him again.

Elizabeth had also begun to count the days until he arrived.

Now she dressed and went into the kitchen. Snow lay in soft piles on the lawn and trees. It was really beautiful, if a person didn't have to go out in it. The forecast called for more snow. Of course Dan wouldn't bother coming up. He would be foolish to risk the trip.

"It looks like we'll spend Thanksgiving with each other again this year," she said to Misty, who was curled up near the floor heat vent. "It won't be the first time, will it?" Misty glanced up at her and twitched an ear, then stretched and yawned. "Yes, I can see you're as excited about the prospect as I am."

Pouring water into the coffee maker, Elizabeth began making her breakfast.

She thought of all the baking and preparations she had done, looking forward to having Dan there.

Up until now, her holidays had been little more than extended weekends. She rarely went anywhere, content to stay at home. It was only after meeting Dan that Elizabeth had discovered a restlessness stirring within her, as though something were missing in her daily routine.

She didn't want to get attached to him. There was no reason to think the marriage would continue after the baby was born. Of course, once the baby had arrived, she would have a child to occupy her time and thoughts. She already knew herself well enough to know that someone like Dan Morgan would not be interested in her as a person. He saw her as the mother of his child and she realized that in that respect she was very important to him.

He really wanted this baby. She rubbed her abdomen and smiled. This was one child who would be greeted with two loving parents. Not like her, handed over at birth before any details could be discovered about her natural parents. Even the name her natural mother had given at the hospital was phony, as well as the address.

Nothing like that would ever happen to her baby, she knew that with a certainty. Carrying her breakfast dishes to the sink, she decided to buy some baby patterns and try her hand at sewing. She might even try to make an afghan. That was as good a way to occupy her long weekend as anything she could think of.

Elizabeth drove to work very carefully, thankful that her street had been cleared and that she wasn't far from the campus. She tried very hard not to think about her disappointment with the weather.

Of course Dan wouldn't come up, no matter what he had said the night before.

As soon as she arrived home after class that afternoon Elizabeth decided to call Dan. There was no reason to sit and wonder if he was coming.

She was unable to reach him. His secretary explained that he was meeting with a client and wasn't expected back to the office that afternoon.

She pictured Dan sitting with an attractive woman, going over ad layouts, and almost laughed at her imagination. What if he was? She certainly had no ties on him, regardless of their legal situation. Their understanding was clear. He was there for her if she needed him with regard to the pregnancy. But that was all.

He had never acted as though he minded giving up his social life because of their marriage. Perhaps because he hadn't actually given it up. Granted, he called each evening. But there was no reason to suppose he stayed at home once he hung up the phone.

Stop it! She was behaving like a possessive, jealous wife, which was certainly not the case. She had no reason to feel possessive or jealous. And she had no idea how it felt to be a wife. A real wife. A wife who was loved and cared for, held in esteem.

When Elizabeth finally went to bed that night she was resigned to spending the rest of the week alone. The snow had never stopped falling, and the traveler's advisories were suggesting that people stay home unless it was an emergency.

She wasn't sure what woke her up later. According to the clock, it was a little past eleven. There was no sound on the street. Elizabeth lay there for a moment, listening. As she turned over restlessly, trying to fall asleep once again, she heard a noise.

She felt around the bottom of the bed and discovered that Misty was no longer in bed with her. No doubt she had found something to play with and was batting it around in the other room, but Elizabeth knew she wouldn't get any more sleep until she investigated.

When she came out of her bedroom she saw the kitchen light was on. Misty had never bothered with light switches and no self-respecting burglar would be so bold. So it must be—

"Hello, Beth. I was afraid I'd wake you up." Dan stood there in his stocking feet, his heavy boots lying beside the chair. Never had his smile been more beguiling.

She realized she was standing there in her bare feet, in an old flannel gown that was warm but far from glamorous. She was so happy to see him she couldn't think of anything to say.

A cold draft of air seemed to circulate around the room and she shivered slightly. "How did you manage to get here?"

"Followed a snowplow. Sorry it took so long."

She couldn't believe he was actually there. Elizabeth forced herself to sound relaxed and offhand. "I didn't expect you to come."

He had picked up his boots and started carrying them over toward the back door, where a rubber mat lay, when she spoke. He stopped and glanced back at her.

"I told you I'd be here."

"That's before the storm blew in."

He dropped his boots and went over to the coffee-pot. Quickly measuring coffee and water, he said, without looking up, "It isn't unusual to have snow-storms at this time of year, you know."

She fought the urge to throw herself into his arms and hold him, just to make sure he was real. "I thought you would change your mind about coming," she offered in a noncommittal tone of voice.

His steady gaze met hers for a moment in silence. "Is that what you hoped?"

She felt the tension building between them. Of course that wasn't what she had hoped, but she didn't want to embarrass him with her eagerness to see him.

"No, of course not." She smiled. "I'm just surprised you managed to get here, that's all."

She looked like a young girl to Dan, in her long flannel gown and her hair done in a single braid. Bare toes peeped out at him, and he realized she hadn't stopped to put on her slippers.

"Don't you think you should get some shoes on? That is, if you intend to stay up for a while."

She glanced down at her feet. Now that he was here she was wide-awake. Without a word she disappeared down the hallway.

Dan glanced over at Misty, who had met him at the door when he arrived.

"I sincerely hope you've been taking your duties as official watch cat seriously. Has she been eating all right? Getting enough sleep? What do you think?"

Misty stared back at him without blinking, and he smiled. "If you know, you certainly aren't going to tell, are you?"

When Elizabeth returned the coffee was ready, and he poured out the brew, placing the cups on the table.

"I tried to call you today," she mentioned, trying to sound casual, "but your secretary said you weren't there and she didn't expect you back."

"Did you tell her who you were?"

"No. I didn't think it mattered."

"Of course it mattered. She has standing instructions to give you my exact whereabouts and a phone number if you should ever call."

She could feel a warm glow begin to swell within her at his words and tone. "Well, it wasn't important, really. I was just going to tell you about the storm and suggest that you might not want to drive up until it cleared."

"Then I'm glad you didn't reach me, since I would have ignored your advice, anyway."

"I'm glad you're here," she murmured.

He had been studying his coffee, and glanced up at her when she spoke. Her cheeks were flushed, either from sleep or from his presence. He wasn't sure what he hoped might have caused the tension he sensed within her. He didn't want to upset her, but he also wasn't going to let her talk him out of their spending time together.

"So am I." He leaned back in his chair and stretched his arms high over his head. "It's been a long day."

"When did you leave?" She tried to ignore the way his sweater tightened across his chest, and forced herself to meet his gaze. She was surprised to discover him watching her intently.

"Sometime around six. My meeting ran over and traffic held me up. I thought about calling to let you know, but by the time I remembered I hadn't called I was already on my way."

She smiled at the frustration she heard in his tone.

"You should sleep warm enough," she offered. "There's an electric blanket on your bed."

He lifted his brow slightly. "*My* bed?"

She flushed. "Well, uh, yes. I aired the guest room for you."

He studied her for a moment in silence. "I see."

"I'm afraid my bed isn't as large as yours and I've been a little restless lately. I wouldn't want to keep you awake."

"Heaven forbid," he responded dryly.

"I'm being silly, aren't I?" she finally asked.

"Not really. You just have a habit of surprising me every so often, that's all. I will be more than willing to sleep wherever you want me." He shoved his chair back and stood up. "As a matter of fact, I could almost fall asleep here at the table." He walked over and placed his cup in the sink, then reached over and unplugged the coffee maker. "I think it's past time for both of us to be in bed."

As though he had always lived there, Dan checked all the doors to see that they were securely locked, then waited in the hallway until she went into her room.

"See you in the morning," he said gently.

"Yes." Elizabeth absently noted that Misty did not follow her into her room. No doubt she had already decided Dan would make a better bed partner.

As she crawled under the covers, Elizabeth wondered what it would be like to sleep with him on a regular basis. He had already been up when she'd awoken both mornings the time she'd stayed with him in New York. She had been concerned that she might crowd him in her small bed as she had in his large one. He might have found himself on the floor, in that event.

The sound of the shower in the main bathroom drifted into her room and she sighed. She wished she better understood proper etiquette in a situation such as theirs. She certainly wasn't much of a hostess, but she supposed he was used to looking after himself.

We're spending Thanksgiving together. He's really here! A sense of anticipation swept over her—a feeling she hadn't experienced since she had lived with Auntie Em. Elizabeth knew better than to expect too much, of course. He was doing the correct thing, spending the holidays with his wife. It was up to her to see that he wasn't bored.

Dan stood under the shower, feeling somewhat defeated. What had he expected? He had to continually remind himself that she was merely tolerating him in her life because he hadn't given her much choice. Just because she had sounded more warm and friendly on the phone than she appeared to be in person had been no reason for him to get his hopes up.

Besides, they had only been married three weeks. He knew it would take longer than that for them to start building ties of friendship.

If only she didn't affect him so strongly whenever he saw her. Her eyes continued to fascinate him, and his body remembered quite well the intimacy they had shared. If it weren't for the fact that he knew she was pregnant, he would almost swear she was still innocent. She had such an untouched air about her, as though she had been locked away from life.

Well, he had knocked down all the walls by his careless action and it was up to him to protect her now.

If she would let him.

Chapter Six

The smell of freshly brewed coffee and frying bacon wafted into Elizabeth's consciousness the next morning, adding to the sense of well-being that her dreams had left with her.

Now that she was awake she could no longer remember the dream, but she had felt safe, secure and very loved. She stretched, rolled over and found a cup of hot coffee sitting beside the bed.

Glancing over at the door, she saw Dan leaning against the doorjamb with his hands in his pockets, watching her.

"Good morning," he said with a half smile.

"You're up early," she managed to mumble.

"I know. It's too nice a day to stay in bed. I thought we might go for a walk after breakfast and enjoy the day," he said, looking out the window.

Bright sunshine caused the snow to sparkle, and the trees glistened with an icy brilliance that almost hurt her eyes.

"Looks like the storm decided not to hang around," he said when she didn't say anything.

Elizabeth wasn't used to waking up and finding someone in her room. It was very disconcerting. She forced herself to act with a semblance of nonchalance and reached for the coffee.

"Thank you for room service."

"My pleasure."

"Have you been up long?"

"About an hour. Misty has kept me company."

"I should have warned you to shut your door. She feels as though she can sleep wherever she pleases."

"She won't get an argument from me. Breakfast should be ready in about ten minutes. Is that okay?"

"Certainly. I'll be right there." He nodded and walked out of the room.

When he'd brought the coffee to her, he was once again mesmerized by the sweet innocence of her face. She had been curled up on her side, her hand under her cheek, her long lashes sweeping over softly tinted cheeks. A slight smile curved her mouth and it had been all he could do to refrain from kissing her.

Easy does it, fellow, he reminded himself. *One wrong move and she won't even accept your phone calls.*

He supposed this weekend was as good a time as any to practice patience. *Think of all the character you're building,* he decided, amused at the thought.

As tired as he'd been, Dan had found himself lying awake for hours the night before, trying to decide the best tack to take with Beth.

By the time he fell asleep, he'd decided to behave as though their marriage were perfectly normal, with one notable exception—they didn't share a bedroom.

His smile was warm and welcoming when Elizabeth joined him in the kitchen.

"Blue is a very becoming color for you," he offered casually, placing her plate of food in front of her.

Elizabeth glanced down at the sweater she had on. Janine had given it to her for Christmas the year before and she seldom wore it, the royal blue was so bright.

"It matches your eyes," he added with a grin.

"Thank you." All his clothes looked fantastic on him. She had a hunch he already knew that.

They made plans over breakfast, and because of Dan's relaxed manner Elizabeth found herself relaxing in turn. He continued to treat their situation as though it were normal, which helped.

During the next four days they enjoyed each other's company. Dan accompanied her to see the doctor and asked interested, discerning questions. After the initial awkwardness of introductions, Elizabeth had little to do but listen to the men discuss her pregnancy.

Dan took her to dinner Saturday, teasing her about eating leftover turkey for the remainder of the year.

He treated her with an unobtrusive protectiveness that she found rather endearing.

And when he got ready to leave on Sunday evening, Elizabeth discovered she had to fight a tendency to burst into tears. No doubt her emotional behavior had something to do with her pregnancy.

"How would you like to spend Christmas with me?" he asked just before he left.

"How long would you want me to stay?"

"As long as you wished."

"What about Misty?"

"Can't you bring her?"

"I suppose, if you don't mind."

"Since she's part of the family, I don't see an alternative, do you?" he asked with a smile.

Part of the family. Elizabeth felt a slight tingle at his words. She'd never been part of a family, but had always been the one looking on. She grinned.

"I've never had her away from home before. There's no predicting how she'll behave."

"We can practice teaching her manners, then."

For the first time since he'd arrived Dan walked over to Elizabeth and carefully slid his arms around her. "Are you going to be okay between now and then?"

She tried to ignore her reaction to his being close, but it was difficult. The scent of his after-shave and the touch of his warm hands on her back affected her strongly. She forced herself to concentrate on his question. "Of course."

"Will you call me if you need anything?"

"I'm sure I won't need to."

He tightened his arms around her for a moment, then relaxed slightly and began to massage her stiff spine. "Call if you just want to chat, okay? I've been the one calling all the time. It would be nice to hear from you, too."

"I hate to bother you. I know how busy you are."

"Never too busy for you. And the next time you call, you make sure my secretary knows who you are, understand?"

She nodded.

He could feel her slowly begin to relax, her body resting against his. Dan felt that his patience over the past few days definitely needed a reward. Surely she wouldn't think he wanted more from her if he indulged in a kiss now that he was leaving.

She had placed her hands on his chest as though prepared to push him away, but now her hands had slipped up to his shoulders, where she absently stroked the hair round his neck and ears.

"Will you kiss me goodbye, Beth? I always seem to be the one kissing you." His voice was low and she quivered slightly at its husky tone.

Going up on tiptoe, she carefully placed her lips on his. They felt firm and yet they easily molded themselves to hers. Elizabeth discovered she enjoyed kissing Dan. She soon became absorbed in the pleasurable activity.

He could feel her breasts pressing against him and it was all he could do not to reach down and touch them. How many times had he lain in bed thinking about her—how beautiful she looked, how warm and inviting—but he forced himself to allow his hands full play on her back only.

Elizabeth felt as though she were drowning in sensation. His exploring tongue gave her a sense of being possessed and she tightened her hold around his neck. She became aware of his hard body closely molded to hers and the effect their kiss was having on him.

For the first time in her life, Elizabeth enjoyed the knowledge that someone wanted her, even if it was only an elemental need.

Pausing to catch her breath, she buried her face in his sweater for a moment.

Attempting a lightness he was far from feeling, Dan managed to say, "Now why couldn't I have gotten a reception like that? Are you so pleased that I'm leaving that you want to give me a rousing send-off?"

She laughed a little raggedly. "I just wanted you to know I enjoyed your being here."

"Well, believe me, I'm not complaining." He kissed her ear, along her jawline and softly touched her lips with his once more. "I enjoyed being with you, too. You're a very special person."

She opened her eyes and stared at him in surprise. "Oh, no. I'm perfectly ordinary, you know."

"Whatever you are, I'm glad I found you."

"We certainly started our relationship off in a rather unorthodox manner," she pointed out.

His eyes sparkled. "So we did. Whoever said a courtship had a set of rules that had to be followed?"

"Is this a courtship?" She had begun to tremble at his words.

"I'm doing my best, Mrs. Morgan, although admittedly I'm out of practice."

She slid her hands down from his neck and absently stroked the muscled surface of his chest. "It isn't really necessary, you know. I understand how you must feel about everything that has happened."

"I doubt that very much. But eventually you may discover that particular piece of information. However, I'm going to insist that you find out on your own, with little to no assistance from me." He carefully set her back from him. "And if I don't get moving, I'll be driving most of the night."

He leaned over for his coat and slipped it on, the collar framing his neck. She reached up and carefully smoothed the collar down, enjoying the softness of the cashmere.

"Somehow I feel as though we've been playing house this weekend. None of it seems real," she admitted a little shyly.

"There's nothing wrong with that occasionally. We both have needed time to adjust to each other and the situation. Don't worry about it."

"You don't feel as though you're being cheated?"

His wicked grin made her wish she had kept her thoughts to herself. "Honey, you just hold that thought and we'll discuss it over Christmas, okay?" He kissed her lightly on the nose, picked up his bag and opened the door. "Don't forget to call."

Elizabeth stood there long after the door had closed and the sound of Dan's car leaving had died away. Why had she suddenly felt the need to clutch him to her?

Misty meowed softly as she brushed against Elizabeth's ankle. She looked down at her. "You're going to miss him, too, aren't you?"

Misty's blue eyed gaze met hers in an unblinking stare.

Elizabeth turned back and walked into her cozy living room. All at once the room, the entire house, seemed empty. How could one person's presence make such a difference?

For the next few weeks Elizabeth kept herself busy, preparing end of the quarter exams and reading the papers handed in. Being alone was something she had always taken for granted. Even when Philip had been a part of her life, she'd grown used to not hearing from him often. They had both been so busy and she had been caught up with her need to gain recognition at the college.

Philip had been comfortable in the background of her life and she had tended to take him for granted. She couldn't imagine ever taking Dan Morgan for granted.

No wonder Philip had wanted out of the relationship. He had been right. She hadn't offered him very much.

Of course she had nothing much to offer Dan, either. Through a quirk of fate she had become the instrument that would give him a child. She couldn't help but wonder if he ever thought of her as anything more than a person who was going to present him with his link to posterity.

As Christmas grew closer she became more and more nervous about her visit. Why hadn't it occurred to her when he suggested it that if she were to visit him they would be sharing the same room and bed? He could have come up there, but would have only been able to stay four days. She wouldn't need to return to school until after the first of the year.

Elizabeth wanted to spend more time with him. That was the reason she had chosen to meet him in Manhattan. She found him fascinating.

Nothing seemed to bother him. He had come to terms with his life and his role in it. Even the thought of having a child and finding himself married to a stranger hadn't seemed to throw him. She wished she could better understand how he managed to be so accepting of their situation.

Her life had suddenly changed direction during the past six months. All her ideas regarding herself and her goals were shifting rapidly. Dan seemed to be the only constant in her life at the moment. She smiled. If she didn't know better, she'd think she had a school-girl crush on the man.

Dan Morgan wearily opened the door to his empty apartment. He'd been pushing himself for the past two weeks, trying to get as much done as possible so that he could spend most of Beth's Manhattan visit with her.

Every night he had to fight the impulse to call and check on her, something he had sworn not to do. He had recognized during his visit upstate that he needed to give her more space. Although she had always sounded pleased to hear from him, he couldn't help but feel that she felt he was pursuing her for some reason.

He *was* pursuing her, but he hoped that he could be subtle enough not to let her become aware of it. Her shocked expression when he'd mentioned courting her had led him to believe she hadn't thought of him in such a guise. So maybe it was better he had backed off.

From now on, he would take his lead from her. Once the baby was born maybe she'd be more receptive to him. Perhaps even learn to trust him.

After a long, relaxing shower Dan crawled into his king-size bed and stretched out with a sigh. She'd be there tomorrow. In his bed.

He smiled, remembering her flannel gown. Not exactly the fantasy garb most men might dream about. He drifted off to sleep, knowing he only had hours to wait.

He doesn't want me to come. That's why he hasn't called since he left in November, Elizabeth decided on the train going south. Of course she could have called him, she reminded herself tartly. But what reason would she have given?

One evening she had tried calling his apartment, but there had been no answer and she refused to try again. She felt better not knowing for sure if he was home.

She'd know by the way he greeted her if he was glad to see her. But, then, he'd always been polite. Did she dare mention how much she had missed his phone calls? Would he think she was making demands on him? He'd already done so much.

Elizabeth was no longer sure what she wanted from him, but she felt such a yearning to see him again. They'd been married a little over seven weeks and he already seemed so much a part of her life. He'd taken over her thoughts, and some of her dreams had made her blush to remember them.

Why hadn't he called her?

He doesn't want me to come.

Her thoughts traveled in circles during the entire train ride from Westfield to Grand Central Station.

The station was crowded when she got there and she had a fleeting thought that he might have forgotten she was coming in that day.

Not that it mattered. She had his address and was certainly capable of finding a cab.

The man in front of her stepped aside, so that she had a better view of the crowd. When she spotted Dan he was shouldering his way through the crowd purposefully, his eyes on her.

Her legs almost collapsed in relief. Of course he was there. He'd said he would be. He pulled her into his arms and hugged her tightly.

"Don't squeeze too hard," she managed to say breathlessly. "He doesn't like to be pushed."

He laughed, a happy, relieved sound that warmed her heart. "So it's a he. When did you discover that?"

She grinned a little sheepishly. "Oh, I didn't find out by any scientific means. He's just been moving around so vigorously I decided referring to him as 'it' seemed to be insulting. He's already got such a personality, I can't think of him as just a being any longer."

He draped his arm around her, protectively guiding her toward the exit. "Can you believe this mob? Everybody is trying to get somewhere else on the Friday before Christmas. I'm sure interplanetary travel isn't half so crowded."

Would he ever let her forget that nonsense?

Dan took Misty's carrying case and pulled Elizabeth close to his side. When they made it outside he looked down at her and said, "You look wonderful." He kissed her on the cheek before helping her into the waiting cab.

"I look fat," she corrected ruefully.

"No way. Your cheeks bloom with health, your eyes sparkle—"

"And I'm gaining too much weight."

"Says who?" he said a little belligerently.

"Me," she responded in a small voice.

He pulled her close in his arms and gave the cabbie an address. "You're just a nice armful." He tilted her chin up and kissed her softly. "I hope you're hungry. I made reservations for dinner a little early so we can get home at a halfway decent hour. We'll swing by my place and I'll let Misty do some exploring while we're gone. It will give her a chance to get acquainted on her own."

"Sounds like a good idea." She couldn't get over how great he looked with his hair windblown and his scarf looped around his neck. He radiated health and vitality and she had never been so glad to see anyone before.

"I'm looking forward to playing house again for a week or so," he said in a low voice.

"Me, too. I've missed you."

"That's news to me. Why didn't you call?"

"I didn't want to bother you. Why didn't you call me?"

"I didn't want to bother you."

They looked at each other for a moment, then began to laugh.

He took her gloved hand in his and tucked it into his coat pocket. "What did the doctor say this time?"

"That I'm healthy and the baby is progressing nicely."

"Has he given you a due date?"

"March 15."

Dan wasn't sure how to phrase his next question. The more he had thought about it, the more he wanted her to stay with him and have the baby in Manhattan, but would she want to change doctors?

Otherwise he knew he would gradually go out of his mind, knowing she was alone. What if she slipped and fell, or needed help and couldn't reach anyone? It didn't bear thinking about.

Somehow during the next couple of weeks he'd have to find a way to broach the subject.

When they arrived at his apartment later that evening Elizabeth felt ready to drop she was so relaxed. The strain of wondering what would happen during this visit and wondering if he still wanted her to come had long since disappeared in a haze of contentment.

Dan had kept her entertained all evening with stories about the advertising agency and some of their clients, and what it was like to work with some colossal egos.

However, on the way home he had become silent and she had sleepily rested her head against his shoulder. She refused to think about the next two weeks. Instead she would enjoy each day as it arrived.

Her eyes opened in surprise when he ushered her into the apartment. Christmas decorations gave a festive air to the room.

"How beautiful! When did you do all of this?"

"Last weekend. I've never bothered with decorations before, since I generally spend my Christmases in California. I decided we needed to get into the spirit of things here."

"Did you tell your sister why you didn't come out this year?"

"Naturally. I said my pregnant wife wasn't up to traveling these days."

Elizabeth tried to decide if he was serious. His crooked smile gave no hint of his thoughts.

"So she knows you're married."

"I saw no reason not to tell her."

"Of course not. Uh, what did she think about the pregnancy?"

"She thought it was way overdue."

"Overdue! That's hardly the case."

"About ten years was her estimate."

"Oh."

"So she's really very pleased with me and said I couldn't have given her a better Christmas present, even if I wasn't going to be there in person. She'd just about given up hope of ever being an aunt."

Elizabeth hadn't given the idea of her child's extended family much thought. Of course her baby would have an aunt, and cousins, even if he didn't have grandparents.

Dan came up behind her and began to knead her shoulders.

"Oh, that feels good," she admitted.

"If you'd like, I'll massage your back tonight."

"Oh, you don't need to bother."

"Believe me, it's no bother. I'd enjoy feeling like I could help. I noticed a couple of times this evening you seemed a little uncomfortable."

"Either you're very observant or I haven't developed a good poker face yet. But I swear he's bowling in there and putting a lot of body English on the ball!"

"Go take a shower and I'll get some lotion."

By the time she was out of the shower, Elizabeth had begun to have second thoughts. If he needed lotion, then he needed a bare body, and she wasn't at all sure she could strip down in front of him, husband or no husband.

She needn't have worried. One small light barely lit the room, and when she gingerly crawled onto her side of the bed, he motioned for her to turn her back to him.

"Relax, try to get the two of you comfortable, and I'll do the rest."

He slid the long length of her gown slowly up until her back, hips and legs were exposed and gently began to massage her muscles.

She forgot to be embarrassed, because his hands felt so good on her tired muscles. No one had ever touched her like that before. In fact, rarely had anyone ever touched her, except for an occasional hug. Even Philip had kept his distance.

Elizabeth drifted off to sleep in a pleasurable haze of sensuous satisfaction, the rhythm of his hands lulling her.

Dan had spent many a night thinking about, and later dreaming about, touching Elizabeth. The present situation was both a pleasure and a torment.

He was delighted to discover that she no longer tensed whenever he touched her. But he wondered if it was just as bad to have her drift off to sleep as though his touch didn't disturb her in the least.

Her satiny skin glowed in the soft light, the gentle curve of her hips accentuating the indentation at her waist. The baby was a small ball in front, leaving her looking very unpregnant from her backside.

Dan had to remind himself that she was indeed very pregnant and that it would do him well to remember that.

Eventually he capped the lotion bottle and turned off the light. Her breathing was steady and quiet. He slipped her gown back down and cautiously curled up to her back. She didn't move.

He let out a sigh of contentment as his hand rested on her stomach. The baby gave a sudden kick and he stroked it gently, wanting to murmur that he meant no harm at all; he just wanted to love both of them.

Dan fell asleep with Beth in his arms. Now that she had arrived, he had everything he could possibly want for Christmas.

Chapter Seven

Elizabeth woke up sometime during the night and discovered that once again she had managed to crowd Dan, although he seemed unaware of it at the moment. Somehow she had managed to place her head on his bare chest. Her leg was thrown over both of his.

The position felt very natural to her. She shifted slightly and discovered that his arm held her firmly to his side.

She felt warm and very content and drowsy. If he was uncomfortable, surely he would complain. Until he did, she decided to enjoy being so close to him.

Elizabeth drifted off to sleep again without moving.

Dan shifted restlessly in his sleep, the evocative scent of Beth's perfume haunting him. His dream had her holding him, loving him. He responded to his dream by drawing her even closer, his mouth searching blindly for hers.

The kiss seemed to last forever. They shared a tenderness, a mutual giving, that seemed to answer the questions, solve the mysteries, explain and summarize their relationship. At last he could touch her as he had wanted to for so long.

His hands found her soft breasts and he lightly touched them, aware of their sensitivity, enjoying their fullness.

A sudden thump vibrated between them and Dan's eyes flew open.

The room was dark except for the lighter square of the window behind his draperies. For a moment he was disoriented, until he realized that the dream wasn't a dream. He held Beth in his arms and his hands had found the warmth of her body.

Their baby had objected to the tight embrace they shared.

"Beth?" he whispered.

"Hmmm?" she mumbled

He smiled, realizing she was still asleep. She certainly responded well in her sleep. Her sleeping position seemed to have become a habit with her, only this time he refused to move away from her. Wasn't this what he wanted, for her to become accustomed to him?

He gently rubbed her rounded stomach. He wanted her right where she was, in his arms. From the looks

of it, at least unconsciously, that's where Beth wanted
to be, as well.

"Good morning." Elizabeth heard his whisper in
her ear before she was fully awake. She started to
stretch, only to discover that she was locked closely
against his side with no way to escape.

Her eyes flew open.

The room was flooded with sunlight and Elizabeth
turned her head slightly on her firm, muscled pillow.

Dan shifted, pushing up on one elbow, so that her
head slipped off his shoulder. She glanced up at him
and saw a very wicked grin and sparkling eyes.

"You once mentioned that I might want something
more from this marriage," he reminded her.

Her heart seemed to be pounding so hard she was
certain he could hear it.

She forced herself to continue to meet his gaze. "Do
you?"

"What do you think?"

From their entwined position Elizabeth had no
doubt how he was affected. The hard, muscled length
of his body pressed against her from shoulder to toe.

"I think I could be in trouble," she admitted with
the hint of a smile.

"You could say that."

He leaned down and kissed her lightly. "However,
I would never want it to be said that I took advantage
of my position."

"You're certainly operating from a very strategic
location, I have to admit."

Since she couldn't move without his compliance, they both understood what she meant.

"Would I be presuming too much, do you suppose, if I decided you wouldn't mind our relationship becoming a little closer?"

She glanced down. "A *little* closer? I don't think we could get much closer than this."

"Oh, I don't know. It might be fun to explore the possibilities."

Elizabeth felt as though she could scarcely catch her breath. None of her thoughts seemed to be connected. They appeared to fly about her head with no semblance of order.

Dan's hands had not been still while he talked. Her gown had somehow become unbuttoned, leaving her rather unprotected from the waist up. His long, sensitive fingers were taking full advantage of that fact.

The baby gave a sudden lurch, effectively breaking the tension that seemed to be mounting between them.

"Good morning to you, too," he said, patting her stomach.

Elizabeth couldn't face what was happening. She felt so misshapen and unattractive. She didn't want Dan to see her like this and yet she didn't want to tell him to stop, either. What a bewildering array of emotions were sweeping through her.

Dan wondered if Beth knew how expressive her face was. Gently he pulled away from her and sat up, trying to ignore his body's protest. "What would you like to do today?" he asked, trying to overcome his shortness of breath.

She wished she knew! Her body and mind seemed to be having a constant war whenever she was around him.

Elizabeth found her gaze following Dan as he slipped out of bed and stood up. A pair of bikini briefs hugged his taut hips and she watched with fascination the way the muscles of his back rippled when he stretched.

He turned around and caught her watching him. She didn't appear to be repulsed by the sight of him, which gave him hope. He sat down on top of the covers, making sure she was warmly tucked beneath them. "Would you like to check out some of the city Christmas decorations, or would the crowds be too much for you?"

She reached out and stroked his face with her fingertips. "I don't think I'd mind a little sight-seeing. It sounds like fun."

Good, he thought with relief. *If we have to spend much time alone here at the apartment, I won't be responsible for losing my grip on my precarious control.*

Elizabeth had never enjoyed a day with so much wholehearted abandonment before in her life. Dan teased her about everything, and they laughed and joked like a couple of kids. More than one person smiled as they passed the two of them, their arms wrapped around each other's waist.

Her fears were forgotten; the uncertain future was pushed away, and Elizabeth delighted in the happiness of the present.

More than one feminine eye noticed Dan as they wandered through the stores and eventually stopped for lunch, Elizabeth noted. He never seemed aware of the attention he received.

Refusing to keep her out so that she got overtired, Dan eventually whisked her back to the apartment and insisted she rest because he had tickets for *The Nutcracker Suite* that evening.

Feeling like a small child, Elizabeth obediently stretched out, knowing she was too keyed up to do more than rest, only to fall into a deep, reviving sleep for more than two hours.

Dan had dinner ready when she woke up so that all she had to do was eat and get ready for the evening. Elizabeth had never felt so pampered in her life.

She tried to put her feelings into words that night. Elizabeth was already in bed when Dan came out of the bathroom, once again wearing only a pair of briefs that left very little to the imagination. He crawled in beside her as though used to finding her in his bed, and then he surprised her by pulling her over to him and resting her head on his shoulder.

"Thank you for today," he said, while he ran his fingers through the silky softness of her hair.

"Oh, Dan. I'm the one who owes you...so many things. You've managed to make Christmas a magical time for me. I'll never forget today...never."

He chuckled and she could feel the rumble where her ear pressed against his chest. "You reminded me of a little girl, your eyes were so wide taking in everything."

"I guess I never realized what this time of the year could really mean to people. It's a time of sharing and giving."

"I know. It's a yearly reminder of love and the wondrous things that love brings to people's lives, if they'll accept it."

She snuggled closer to him, smoothing her hand across his chest, enjoying the tactile sensation. "In recent years I've managed to treat the holidays as a vacation from school and tried not to think about how other people spent them."

He lifted her chin and pressed his lips gently against hers. "Now we can start some family traditions of our own, can't we?"

Her heart leaped at his gesture and his words. His suggestion had such a sense of permanency and it touched her deeply.

"That's true. We can," she managed to respond.

They lay there together in contented silence. Elizabeth had almost drifted off to sleep, when Dan spoke again.

"Are you sorry you married me?"

His question surprised her. "Of course not. Why do you ask?"

"Because I didn't give you much choice, as I recall."

"I'll admit the idea took some getting used to. And I'm not at all sure I really feel married. Not with our present living arrangements."

She couldn't have given him a better opening.

"Why don't you stay here, then? They're going to have to replace you this spring, anyway. Then we'd have some time together before the baby gets here."

Elizabeth couldn't think of anything she'd enjoy more. "Are you sure I wouldn't be in the way?"

He laughed, a relieved, relaxed sound that made her smile. "Do you look like you're in the way?" He allowed his hands to rest lightly on her back and side, as though enjoying having her in his arms. "We could find a larger place, if you'd like."

She looked around the darkened room. "I like this place."

"So do I, for now. But the baby will need a room of his own eventually."

Once again Elizabeth heard the intention of permanency in what he was saying. Would it be possible to build a marriage on the unusual basis with which this one had started? At that moment, she felt as though anything were possible if a person could only believe in it.

Dan shifted, turning to her, and Elizabeth could feel the tension in his body. "I want to make love to you so much." His husky voice emphasized his need.

He kissed her. It was a kiss of claiming and possession, of longing and intensity. Nothing else mattered at the moment.

For a second, Elizabeth felt a panicky feeling of inadequacy. She knew so little about expressing herself. She wanted Dan to know how much he meant to her and that she was willing to deepen the relationship. Could she show him?

He slipped her gown off carefully, then began to explore her softness with a gentleness that told her more than anything he could have said in words that he would never rush her or take advantage of their relationship.

Dan felt her response to him and it was as though a weight had been lifted from him. As private a person as Beth was, he knew she wouldn't be willing to share herself without trusting him.

She appeared to be with him during each successive step toward intimacy. He refused to rush her. Instead he luxuriated in her touch as she hesitantly imitated him as he explored her.

Then he felt her stiffen and he paused. His mouth had found her breast and he immediately pulled back, afraid he'd hurt her.

"I'm sorry. I didn't mean to hurt you."

"You didn't. I mean—I'm not sure what it is, but—"

Her voice sounded frightened and he could feel an inner alarm going off. It wasn't a fear of lovemaking that caused the panicky tone in her voice.

"What is it, Beth?"

"I think it's the baby," she whispered.

"What about the baby?"

"I had a pain in my abdomen. A sharp pain."

Dan tried not to panic. It wasn't time for the baby. It was much too soon.

He sat up and turned on the light. Elizabeth looked pale, her eyes wide in her face. He tried to sound calm.

"Why don't I take you over to the hospital emergency and let them check you, all right?"

"It's probably nothing. They'll think we're being silly."

"I don't particularly care what they think. I'd be pleased to discover it's nothing, believe me. But I don't want you getting upset."

While he talked Dan began to throw on his clothes. Then he reached into his closet and found one of her maternity dresses. He laid it on the bed. "Do you feel up to getting dressed?"

Gingerly she crawled out of bed and reached for her clothes.

Dan called the lobby of his building and asked them to have a cab waiting, then he helped her finish dressing. He hoped it was nothing. *Please let it be a gas pain or too much excitement. Don't let anything be wrong with the baby.*

The hospital staff immediately took over in a quiet, efficient manner as soon as Dan and Elizabeth arrived. The doctor in charge had her change into a gown for an examination, while Dan waited out in the hallway.

"The waiting room is just down the corridor, sir," one of the nurses pointed out.

"No. I want to be here, in case she calls for me."

The nurse smiled. "I'm sure she's going to be all right."

"Does that come in the form of a written guarantee?"

She shook her head. "Is this your first baby?"

"Yes."

"Don't worry. These unexplained pains come without any rhyme or reason. They don't necessarily mean anything."

When the doctor came out of the examining room Dan was still waiting in the hall. The doctor nodded and said, "The baby seems to be all right, Mr. Morgan. However, I have told Mrs. Morgan that she should make plans to spend as much time off of her feet as possible between now and her delivery date."

"What's wrong?"

"Just a precaution. There's no reason to alarm either of you. I'm just saying that sensible precautions will ensure that nothing goes wrong."

Dan thought about how close they had come to making love and it scared him. They didn't dare take any risks. "May I take her home now?"

"I don't see why not. She'd much prefer to spend Christmas at home, I'm sure."

By the time they got back to the apartment, Elizabeth was laughing. "Dan, you don't have to treat me as though I'm going to break, you know. The doctor said I probably did too much today. I'm not used to so much activity."

"Beth, will you call the school and explain to them that you're going to stay here with me? There's no way I'm going to let you out of my sight until that baby arrives safely."

"Who are you going to hire to run the agency while you sit and watch me?"

"Now you're making fun of me."

"Not at all. If you like, I'll teach you to crochet. We can sit here together and make baby clothes and watch daytime television."

She began to laugh even harder at the look on his face. "Yes, I'll call the school, Dan. I had already decided I'd like to stay before everything started to happen."

When they returned to bed, Dan deliberately shifted to his own side. He was not going to take any chances. "Good night, Beth."

Elizabeth turned on her side, trying to find a comfortable position. "Good night, Dan. I'll try not to keep you awake."

"No problem. If you have any more pains, tell me."

"Okay."

"Beth?"

"Hmmm."

"Take care of yourself, please."

"I have been."

"I know. I just don't want anything to happen to you or the baby."

The warm tenderness in his voice brought tears to her eyes.

"Nothing will happen. But since I'm supposed to take it easy, and tomorrow is Christmas Eve, maybe we should cancel our plans to go out."

"Absolutely. It will be nice to have a quiet evening at home." *If I can remember to keep my hands off of you,* he thought with a pang.

Elizabeth lay awake long after Dan's even breathing convinced her he was asleep. They had so nearly made love tonight and she had wanted it to happen. Perhaps it was just as well something had prevented it.

While lying in the examining room, waiting for the doctor, Elizabeth had come face to face with the fact that she was in love with Dan. The thought scared her. She didn't want to love him. She was afraid to become that attached to anyone, but love hadn't given her a choice.

She would have to come to terms with how to handle her feelings and wait to see how he felt for her. Just because he wanted to make love with her didn't mean he loved her. She understood that. Wouldn't it be wonderful, though, if he could fall in love with her, too? She drifted off to sleep trying to imagine what their life together could be.

Chapter Eight

Within a few weeks, Elizabeth felt comfortable with her new routine. The college had understood her concern for her pregnancy and arranged for her to have the necessary time off.

For the first time in her life, Elizabeth discovered that she could enjoy playing the role of housewife, at least on a temporary basis.

She had breakfast prepared each morning by the time Dan had showered and dressed. At first he protested, insisting she needed her rest and that he was used to preparing his own meals. Elizabeth explained that she had nothing else to do but rest after he left, and she enjoyed spending those few minutes each morning with him. The warm look he gave her made her pulse race and he agreeably sat down and ate the meal she prepared that first morning, and, after that, never said another word about her getting up when he did.

After he left each day, she straightened the apartment. He absolutely refused to let her do the heavy cleaning after explaining she had no business stooping and bending when she was alone and couldn't get help if she needed it.

So Elizabeth stopped feeling guilty about spending so much time reading and making clothes for the baby.

She had been in Manhattan almost three weeks when she called Janine at work.

"Well, hello, stranger," Janine said after Elizabeth identified herself. "You're a hard person to catch at home. I've tried calling you several times, but could never get an answer."

Elizabeth had told Janine the day of her wedding that she would continue to teach, so it was natural that Janine had assumed she was still in Westfield. There was so much to explain to her friend.

"Actually, that's why I called. I'm here in Manhattan and wondered if you would like to meet me for lunch."

"Let me check my calendar real quick here," Janine replied. Elizabeth could hear pages flipping. "I just got back to town yesterday. You should see my desk! Oh, good, I don't have anything down until two-thirty. Why don't we meet at the little place across from my office at one? It will be great to see you again!"

Elizabeth dressed with special care. There was no way to hide her condition, but she wanted to look as attractive as possible.

She made certain that she arrived first and found a table so that she could watch for Janine. When she came sailing through the door a few minutes later, Elizabeth waved, then watched her friend weave her way through the crowded restaurant.

"God, you look ravishing," were Janine's first words when she sank into the chair across the table from Elizabeth. "Marriage obviously agrees with you."

Elizabeth laughed. "I believe you're right. I've never felt better in my life."

Janine busied herself removing her gloves and coat, then picked up the menu. "I wonder what the special is today? I'm starved."

As usual Janine looked slender and elegant, every inch the successful businesswoman. Elizabeth hadn't realized how much she had missed talking with her.

Janine glanced up. "What are you planning to have? You never have to worry about your weight...." Her words faded away as she took a closer look at the dress Elizabeth wore. "Beth?" Her eyes widened. "Aren't you wearing—I mean, isn't that a— Are you—?"

At that moment the waitress arrived to take their order. The interruption gave Elizabeth some time in which to respond. She had never seen her former roommate at a loss for words and was more amused than discomfited now that the time to tell her had come. "The word is pregnant, Janine," she said, once the waitress departed. "And yes, I am going to have a baby," she added gently, enjoying the shocked expression on her friend's face.

"But that's awful! I mean, you haven't been married long. And your job? What are you doing about your job? And Dan. How does he feel about it? Oh, Beth—" she reached over and took her friend's hand and clasped it between hers "—I'm so sorry," she murmured in a bereaved tone.

Elizabeth burst out laughing. She couldn't help it. Janine was so obviously stricken. To Janine and her life-style, a pregnancy would no doubt represent catastrophe. Elizabeth could understand and empathize with her reaction, but she also had to let Janine know her own feelings about the matter.

"I'm delighted with my pregnancy," Elizabeth replied. "Dan seems to be taking it in stride. I'm living here in Manhattan now, as a matter of fact. He didn't like the idea of my living alone in Westfield."

Janine studied her friend for a moment. "Well, I must admit you're certainly glowing. I've never seen you more beautiful."

Elizabeth flushed slightly. "Thank you."

"So when is this blessed event to take place?"

Elizabeth had hoped she wouldn't be asked a direct question. She also knew she would not lie. There was no point. Sooner or later Janine would know the truth.

"Mid-March."

"March! But Beth—"

Janine's words were cut off so quickly it seemed as though an invisible hand had clamped across her mouth. She sat there for a moment, and from her expression Elizabeth could tell that Janine was rapidly putting all the pieces together. She had always known that Janine had a quick mind. She was once again reminded of that fact.

"How did Dan know?" were her first words.

"What do you mean?"

"How did he know to search for you? When I talked to him the first time he said you hadn't told him your name, where you lived or what you did for a living."

"That's true."

"Then how did he know you were pregnant?"

"He didn't."

The waitress appeared with their meals, placing the dishes silently in front of the two women. Janine studied Elizabeth in silence for a moment, then sighed. She looked tired and somehow defeated.

"What's wrong?" Elizabeth asked, after sampling a bite of food.

"Nothing, really. It's just that every time I think I've broken through your barriers and that we've become close friends, I find another barrier I never knew existed."

"Janine, you're the closest friend I've got. You know me better than anyone."

"That's what disheartens me so. You never mentioned a thing to me about that night, what happened or what followed later, when you discovered you were pregnant. That must have been a very traumatic time for you, when you could have used some support. That's what friends are for, honey. And you never said a word.''

"I didn't mean to hurt your feelings."

"I know you didn't. You're just used to facing the world alone. You've never depended on anyone else in your life."

"That's because there was never anyone to depend on."

"Maybe not, when you were a child. But once you were older, I was there, then Philip and now—"

"And now there's Dan," Elizabeth finished for her.

"Yes," Janine said thoughtfully. "There's Dan. He didn't strike me as the type to come on so strong the first time you met. He struck me as the type my mother used to describe as a perfect gentleman."

Elizabeth could feel her face burning. "He is. And he was." She forced herself to meet her friend's amused gaze. "Truly, he was."

"Well, honey, I don't think a true gentleman gets a girl pregnant on their first date."

"Janine!" Elizabeth glanced around them, desperately hoping that none of the other people in the busy restaurant had heard her.

"Sorry. I didn't mean to shock you," Janine teased. "All I'm saying is that I'm surprised at both of you."

"So was I. That's why I didn't tell you the next day. I was too embarrassed."

Janine laughed. "Oh, Beth, I adore you—you're so refreshing. Embarrassed, of all things."

"Well, how did you think I would feel about it? All the time I was with Philip and he never... We didn't— Then I meet Dan and—" She waved her hand helplessly.

"Did Dan know you were a virgin?"

Elizabeth glanced around hurriedly, then leaned across the table. "Would you mind lowering your voice? There's no reason to make an announcement to everyone in the room!"

Janine's eyes sparkled at the reprimand. In a whisper she said, "Well, did he?"

"We never discussed it. Neither one of us intended for it to go that far. It just happened. I really can't explain it."

"Is that why you married him?"

"I thought so. Now, I'm not so sure."

"What do you mean?"

"He made a very convincing argument that he deserved to help raise his child and marriage made a logical step toward being able to do that, but— Oh, I don't know. I can't see myself marrying anyone I didn't care for. I look back even now and I'm amazed at what happened the night we met. It seemed so unreal—like a fantasy or something enchanted."

"Some enchanted evening, huh? I believe it's already been done in song," Janine quipped.

"Well, whatever it was, Dan has a powerful effect on me. I agreed to marry him, and until the baby is born, I agreed to quit work and live here with him."

"Sounds like love to me," Janine said with a grin.

"I know," Elizabeth replied softly.

"It couldn't happen to a nicer person, you know. You deserve a little happiness and I'm pleased as punch for you."

Elizabeth grinned. "So am I. Sometimes I can't believe it's me. We seem to be so relaxed with each other, and I enjoy his wry sense of humor. He doesn't seem to get uptight about anything."

"With the luscious Beth in bed with him every night, I'm sure he manages to work out all of his tensions."

Elizabeth seemed to find the contents of her glass all engrossing. She didn't raise her eyes when she replied. "Actually, we haven't made love since that first night." When Janine didn't say anything Elizabeth finally glanced up. Her friend's astonished expression caused her to chuckle.

"I've never heard a stranger tale in my life," Janine finally managed to say.

"That was the arrangement when we first decided to marry, you see, and . . . well . . ."

"And he's never made any overtures toward you that he might want the arrangement changed?"

Elizabeth wished she could discuss the situation without blushing. After all, this was Janine, who had shared with Elizabeth the details of every romance she'd ever had. So why should Elizabeth be so shy with her now?

"Well, Dan is a very affectionate person, so he holds me and kisses me frequently."

"Good for Dan," Janine commented dryly. "For a moment there you really had me worried. Does Dan seem to mind that there's so little to your, uh, sex life?''

"Not that I can tell, but what do I know about men? He's very patient with me, loving and kind—"

"Trustworthy and loyal. Dear Lord, Beth, you make him sound like a Boy Scout.''

Elizabeth grinned. "He probably was at one time, now that you mention it.''

"No doubt." Janine leaned back in her chair. "Well, whatever he's doing seems to be working. You're obviously happy.''

Elizabeth nodded. "I am."

"So what's going to happen when the baby arrives? Will you go back to teaching? Live here in Manhattan? What?''

"I intend to resume teaching this fall. I'm not sure how that will work out as far as Dan is concerned. He says to take one step at a time, that we will work something out. Who knows? He may prefer a long distance relationship once the reality of a demanding baby hits him.''

"Somehow I doubt that," Janine said slowly. "Something tells me that Dan Morgan understands his priorities and I have a strong hunch you and that baby are at the top of his list.''

Elizabeth's expression grew dreamy. "I hope so.''

Dan came home early that afternoon and found Elizabeth asleep. For a moment his heart seemed to stop. Was she not feeling well? He walked over to the bed and leaned over.

Elizabeth opened her eyes and saw him. Her spon-
taneous smile encouraged him greatly. Glancing at the
clock, she sat up and put her arms around his neck.
"You're home early," she said, kissing him.

He sat down beside her and pulled her into his lap,
his mouth never leaving hers. When they finally
paused for breath, both of them were a little shaken.

"Maybe I'd better come home early more often, if
I'm going to get that sort of welcome."

"I always kiss you hello."

"I know. But there's something about you all warm
and cuddly from sleep that I find particularly arous-
ing." He looked at her closely. "Are you feeling all
right?"

"Oh, I'm fine. I just ate too much for lunch and it
made me sleepy, so I came home and decided to take
a nap."

"Did you go shopping?"

"Oh, no. I met Janine for lunch. It's the first time
I've seen her since we got married."

Dan looked at her with a speculative gleam in his
eye. "No doubt she noticed your new shape."

"Indeed she did."

"And?"

"And what?"

"Aren't you going to tell me her reaction?"

"Oh, about what you'd expect. Surprised, pleased
for me."

She sounded very relaxed and casual, and Dan decided that she had come a long way in her attitude in
the weeks since they married. He still held her to him,

enjoying the closeness, pleased to see how naturally she accepted his embrace. His campaign was definitely showing progress.

He helped her with dinner, a simple meal that didn't take long to prepare. Dan told her about his day while they ate, making the story amusing so he could enjoy watching her whenever she laughed.

Having her in his life had changed his perspective about everything—his business, his goals and his enjoyment of life. He found himself eager to come home, to be with Beth, to watch her laugh, see her smile, and to hold her close to him in the still, quiet darkness of the night.

"Did Janine mention Ryan today?" he asked.

"No. Most of our conversation was about the baby."

"I wonder if they're seeing each other?" he mused.

"When would they have time, with Janine on the West Coast so much? And didn't someone mention that Ryan travels a great deal as well?"

"Yes, he does. Too bad they don't coordinate their schedules so they might end up in the same city at the same time occasionally."

They smiled at each other. "We sound like a typical pair of matchmakers, don't we?" Elizabeth commented.

Dan stood up and stretched. "That we do. Neither one of them would appreciate our efforts, if they knew." He rubbed his neck wearily.

"Does your neck hurt?"

"It's just a little stiff."

"Why don't you go stand under a hot shower and see if that helps? If not, I'll massage it for you." She stood up and started to clean off the table.

"You don't have to do that."

She smiled at him. "I know. But I also know how good a massage feels."

Later, when he came out of the shower he found her waiting for him. She was in her voluminous nightgown that made her look about ten years old.

She crawled into bed and patted the place next to her. He didn't need to be coaxed. After pouring a small amount of lotion on her hands, she briskly rubbed them together to warm the liquid. Then she began to apply it to his neck and shoulders in long, smooth strokes.

Dan groaned his appreciation.

Elizabeth had never been given the opportunity to touch him so freely. Although she had never given him a massage before, she had learned a little of the technique from the ones he gave to her.

As she kneaded the muscles in his neck, she felt him relax. Elizabeth smiled to herself. She knew how good that must feel. She was enjoying it, as well. The muscled plane of his shoulders sloped into the slim line of his spine. Her hands followed the contours of his body, from his broad shoulders down to his narrow waist.

Elizabeth had never realized how much enjoyment could be derived from touching someone. Was that why Dan seemed to find so many reasons to touch her?

Living with Dan was quite an education for her. She wondered how he felt about their arrangement. He never said and she didn't want to make an issue of it.

She noticed that he was asleep. Reaching over she turned off the light and settled down on the pillow next to him. He turned over, pulling her into the curl of his body and placed his hand over the baby. The baby thumped an acknowledgment.

"Good night, you two," he murmured into her ear.

"Good night," she whispered, feeling at peace in the circle of his arms.

Chapter Nine

By mid-February Elizabeth felt as though she had spent her entire life pregnant and ugly. Not being able to teach had begun to make the days drag by. She was tired of reading and bored with sewing. Trying to be cheerful and good company to Dan when he was home had brought out a hitherto unsuspected acting ability that had surprised her.

She had vowed to herself that Dan would not be made to suffer for what, after all, was her problem. For some reason her body hadn't adapted well to the pregnancy. The doctor she'd found in Manhattan had been optimistic that she could carry the baby full term with plenty of rest and care. She was basically healthy. A little narrow in the pelvic area, perhaps, but he had assured her that complications could be kept to a minimum with her cooperation.

She cooperated with a grim determination. Part of her determination was to convince Dan that everything was all right in her little world.

Whenever he was home she never had to pretend. The more she was around him the more she grew to love him.

If only she could have the baby and return to being slender and supple once again. Elizabeth wanted to show him how she felt toward him and how much she appreciated him, but the opportunity never seemed to present itself.

And for the past several weeks he had begun to treat her like a favorite elderly aunt, although he seemed to enjoy her company, keeping her entertained with humorous anecdotes about the business world. In addition, he suggested short outings to keep her from going completely out of her mind.

But he was notably unloverlike.

Elizabeth discovered that she missed his affectionate hugs and kisses. She missed his touch. As she had grown heavier he had gotten into a routine of massaging her back each evening before she went to sleep, but his touch was impersonal.

What could she expect? He was probably appalled at her size and shape. And no wonder. He couldn't be held responsible for not loving her, she could understand that. Elizabeth's daytime fantasies seemed to center around the time when she would look attractive enough to make him aware of her as a woman.

At times she was convinced that would never happen. She would be the only woman in history to spend the rest of her allotted years pregnant.

Dan glanced at his desk calendar. Today was February 20. The baby was due in less than one month. He ran his hand through his hair, creating a ruffled effect, and sighed.

Another month. He reminded himself that he had successfully completed two months during which he'd been with Beth every day—and night—and had managed to keep his hands off of her. For some reason he had thought it would become easier with practice. That certainly hadn't been the case.

She became more delectable with time. He had never seen a pregnant woman move so gracefully—even lightly—before. And her skin glowed with a translucence as though a light were turned on inside her.

He had also noticed a definite softening and tenderness in her eyes whenever she looked at him—which had almost been his undoing on more than one occasion. There were times when he had a definite feeling that she was his just for the taking. Except he couldn't take her, not until after the baby arrived safely.

The back rubs were a nightly form of torture he'd managed to devise for himself during the past several weeks. Never before had he realized the masochistic tendencies in him that must have lain dormant for years. He had actually been the one to suggest them.

They seemed to help her and that was the important thing. And he had gotten used to staying awake most of the night, trying not to think how soft and warm she felt.

At one point during the dark hours he decided that this was his punishment for his behavior the night they met. Because he indulged himself he was now forced to live with her, sleep with her and not make love to her again.

He felt the punishment overly harsh. Then it occurred to him that the worst punishment would have been not to have found her at all, but to have spent his life looking for her.

He'd paused in his furious thoughts and listened to her soft breathing nearby, and smiled. No. It was easier to wait for her and be beside her during the wait.

Cold showers had become a way of life for him.

The phone rang, effectively erasing his frustrated thought.

"Hello?"

"Hi, Dan. You probably don't remember me, but we met last year when you were in California. My name is Selena Stanford."

Not remember Selena Stanford? She must be kidding.

"Of course I remember you, Selena. How is Adam?"

"Couldn't be better. Would there be a chance that we could see you sometime this week? We're flying into New York tomorrow and we're hoping to discuss

an advertising campaign several of us here on the West
Coast would like to launch. Are you interested?''

"I never turn down an offer like that. How long are
you going to be here?''

"Until the weekend. We're not bringing the children, and I don't like to be away from them too long.''

"Why don't you plan to have dinner with me tomorrow evening and we can chat and go from there?
Besides, I'm eager to introduce you to my wife.''

"Your wife! Congratulations, Dan. I hadn't heard
you had gotten married. I think dinner sounds fine.
I'll call you as soon as we get to the hotel, if that's all
right.''

"Sounds good to me. See you tomorrow. Oh, and
Selena?''

"Yes?''

"Thanks for thinking of me.''

"Who are you kidding? When it comes to advertising, yours is the first name on the list. Bye for now.''

Dan hung up the receiver with a smile. Selena Stanford. A big name in show business. He wondered what
sort of advertising she had in mind. She had her own
agent, so it couldn't be personal. Shrugging, he decided to wait and see.

If nothing else, living with Beth had certainly taught
him patience.

"Are you sure you wouldn't prefer a larger apartment?'' Dan asked Elizabeth that night over dinner.
"You must feel very cooped up here. It was never

meant for more than one person and I knew I wouldn't be spending much time here, anyway.''

"Positive. As much as I enjoy Manhattan, I don't want to raise the baby here. The apartment is fine for your needs.''

"You don't intend to stay here once the baby arrives, I take it,'' he said in a careful tone, trying not to sound as though the thought of her leaving panicked him.

She looked at him in surprise. "How can I? It's a little far to commute from here to college.''

"And you intend to teach after the baby comes,'' he commented, making a statement more than asking a question.

"Not immediately afterward of course, but, yes, by next fall I expect to have found a housekeeper.''

"And what about us?''

She hadn't heard that cold tone since he'd first discovered she was pregnant and hadn't intended to tell him. "Does having an 'us,' as you put it, preclude my continuing with my career?''

The candlelight that Beth had added to the table hadn't helped Dan to stay objective about his wife's beauty. The soft glow made her eyes sparkle, and when she looked at him with that level gaze he had an intense desire to grab her and love her until she admitted she didn't want to leave him.

He tamped down those prehistoric man tendencies and tried to be reasonable.

"Of course not. I don't mind commuting. We might look for a home somewhere between here and Westfield, so that getting to and from work wouldn't be too difficult for either one of us.''

She smiled at him, that magical smile that seemed to reach deep down inside of him and tug. ''You must have given the matter some thought.''

He took a sip of his wine and nodded. ''I want to give this relationship every possible chance to work. At the very least we need to live together. It's important to me to have daily contact with the baby.'' *And you,* he added silently.

The baby. Don't forget the purpose of the relationship, Elizabeth reminded herself.

''We'll have time to look before school starts,'' she said agreeably, and Dan felt like cheering. She hadn't said no. He felt like jotting down the date and marking another victory in his campaign to build a permanent—and loving—relationship with the beautiful woman seated across from him.

After that, Dan kept the conversation on lighter subjects and the rest of the evening passed quietly.

''What would I do without you?'' Elizabeth murmured a few hours later while Dan massaged her back and shoulders. ''You've been so good to me.''

''That works both ways, you know. You've been very good to me.''

She twisted her head slightly so she could see him. ''How is that?''

''You've given me something to look forward to in my life, a reason to be putting in the long hours I do. I look forward to coming home to you each evening.'' His hand slowly rubbed across her lower back.

He was glad she was unaware of his pulse rate at the moment. "You're doing a great job of hiding how restrictive you find the pregnancy, and I know how hard that has been for you to accept."

"You weren't supposed to notice."

"Oh, I notice lots of things."

"Even that sounds ominous."

"Are you aware of how little you complain?"

"Misty would argue with you on that point."

"Therefore I have cooked up a little reward for you."

She rolled onto her back so that she could see him. His bland expression gave nothing away. "Oh, really? What's that?"

"I checked with your doctor and he said that if you spent most of tomorrow off your feet I had his permission to take you to dinner tomorrow night. So we have reservations at Maxwell's Plum."

"Oh, Dan, that sounds delightful." She leaned up on one elbow and slid her hand around his neck. "Thank you," she murmured, pulling him toward her until their lips met.

She was breaking Dan's unwritten rule of physical contact, but how could he resist such a warm and loving thanks?

When she drew back a few moments later, they were both a little breathless.

"We'll also have someone with us."

"Ryan and Janine?"

"No. I tried to reach them, but they're both out of town. But there's someone special I want you to meet.

She'll be in town for the next few days and agreed to have dinner with us tomorrow night."

"She?" Elizabeth felt a definite sinking sensation settle over her.

"I've only met her once before, when I was out on the West Coast, but I was very impressed with her. She's never let her success in two different careers stop her from being a very warm and caring person. I know you're going to love her."

With a buildup like that, how can any self-respecting wife do anything but hate the woman on sight, Elizabeth decided wryly. When was the last time she'd heard that tone of warm affection in Dan's voice? *Not since you became pregnant.*

"Who is she?"

"Selena Stanford."

"The movie star? The writer? Oh, Dan, I can't possibly meet her looking like this." She saw the expression of startled surprise on his face and realized how that had sounded. "I mean, I look so fat and awkward and—"

"Selena will certainly understand what you're going through. She has twins, from what I understand."

Elizabeth remembered Selena from a television series she'd co-starred in a few years back. She'd been on a very successful show, then she disappeared for a while. Last spring she was nominated for an Academy Award for a screenplay she'd written. All that talent and looks, too. Elizabeth groaned.

Ordinarily she would be delighted to meet her. But not now. "I can't, Dan. Really."

"I'm having one of the department stores send you over a selection of dresses to choose from so you'll have something different to wear. I thought you'd enjoy getting out, and your doctor felt it might be good for you."

She could hear the tone of concern in his voice and pulled herself up sharply. What was she doing? He wanted to do something for her and here she was acting like a spoiled child. It could have been worse, she supposed. What if he'd wanted her to meet Queen Elizabeth? *Try to keep things in perspective,* she silently reminded herself.

"Of course I'll go, Dan. I'm just being silly. Blame it on the pregnancy. What time should I be ready?"

He was just as concerned over the sudden switch. Now she was being bright and cheerful. Too bright and cheerful. He could see the strain around her eyes and he wished he knew what he could do to help her.

"We should leave here by seven. We'll be meeting them there."

"Them?"

"Selena and Adam, her husband."

"Oh." She gave him a serene smile. "That sounds like fun." With a determined tilt to her chin, she added for good measure, "I can hardly wait."

Dan's first sight of Beth the next evening took his breath away. Her dress was a deep blue that emphasized eyes that didn't need anything to make them memorable. The style of the dress drew attention to her creamy shoulders and drew his eyes to her cleavage, which the pregnancy had enhanced more than his heart would be able to stand, he was certain.

She'd done something exotic with her hair, pulling it up and away from her face, leaving the clean, patrician features glowing beneath expert touches of color.

"You look like a princess," he said, as though unaware he had spoken aloud.

She gave him a modified curtsy. "Thank you, kind sir."

He couldn't take his eyes off of her. She began to smile, and he realized he was staring. "You're like no other woman I've ever known."

Her smile faltered somewhat at the intensity evident in his voice. He shook his head slightly, as though coming out of a daze. "Let me get my shower. I should be ready in twenty minutes or so."

"There's no rush. I just thought I'd be out of your way when you got home."

Out of his way. That was a laugh. He walked into the bathroom and smelled her scent, felt the moist heat that had been generated by her shower and knew that tonight was going to be a subtle form of torture.

Elizabeth had seen Dan in his business clothes and dressed casually, but she had never seen him looking so striking before. The black suit he wore brought out the blond highlights of his hair and made his eyes gleam with a silver glow. He looked like someone who had stepped out of an advertisement for Caribbean Sea cruises—sensually magnetic.

"Wow!" was her only form of expression to his presence when he walked back into the room.

"Wow?" he questioned. "From an English professor?"

"Literature," she corrected.

"Close enough."

"You're right. Give me a while and I'll try to write an ode to how you look tonight."

He laughed. "I can hardly wait. Are you ready?"

Was she ready to share him with some glamorous and stunning movie star? He must be out of his mind.

"Of course." Her acting abilities continued to astound her.

Smiling, they left the apartment and hailed a cab. Upon arrival at the restaurant they were immediately ushered to their table. Dan ordered them each a glass of wine to enjoy while they waited.

"I've never been here before," Elizabeth commented, taking in the decor and the number of people there.

"As you can tell, it's a popular place. And the food is magnificent." He idly noted that the man two tables over couldn't seem to keep his eyes off of Beth's neckline and he had a strong urge to discuss the matter with him. Selena couldn't have made a more timely arrival, he decided, when he spotted her at the door.

He stood and waited for them to reach the table. "Good to see you again, Selena," he said with a smile. He offered his hand to Adam. "You, too, Adam." The tall man smiled as he took the chair next to his blond and beautiful wife. "This is my wife, Beth... Selena and Adam Conroy," Dan said, finishing the introductions, and sat down.

"I was delighted to hear you had married, Dan,"
Selena said with a mischievous grin. She turned to
Elizabeth. "I certainly admire your taste."

"Behave yourself," Adam said to his wife. "She
may not understand your sense of humor."

Selena's eyes danced. "I'm sure she will. Just as she
knows that wasn't a joke. I'm very sincere," she added
with a wink.

Elizabeth couldn't help but like the irrepressible
Selena, who managed during the course of dinner to
draw her out, little by little. Before Elizabeth could
quite decide how it had happened, she and Selena were
chatting as though old friends—about husbands, ba-
bies and being a celebrity.

"There are times that being a celebrity has its com-
pensations," Selena admitted to the other three as they
drank their coffee after dinner. "And that's when I
want to get an important message to people. At least
they stop and listen, and that's the first step." She set
down her cup and looked at Dan. "That's where you
come in, Dan. I need your help to know how to get
their attention and I knew you'd have some suggestions."

"What's your message?"

"I want to get people involved in the hunger pro-
ject."

"We've certainly become more aware of world
hunger in the past few years," Dan admitted.

"We need to educate the people to face the fact that
each of us is responsible for the situation and that
none of us can turn our back."

"But it's always been there, Selena," Dan pointed out.

"I know. But the time to change their thinking is now, Dan. We need to stop world hunger. It's an idea whose time has come. As soon as a person becomes aware that he makes a difference, whole avenues open up to allow changes—necessary, miraculous changes. There are no limitations to what people can do when they realize their own potential."

"And that's what you want to point out?"

"Yes, in a way that will grab their interest, cause them to find out more about what is being done and how they can help."

"I'd enjoy working with you on some ideas, Selena. I cleared tomorrow's calendar so that we could spend some time together. You can fill me in."

She laughed. "Adam's the one who has all the facts and figures. I knew that photographic mind of his would be invaluable." She glanced at Elizabeth. "In the meantime, if you will excuse me, Beth and I will visit the ladies' room."

As soon as they reached the lounge Selena explained. "I can remember those last few weeks of pregnancy when you seemed to spend more time in the bathroom than anywhere else. Thought you might enjoy a visit."

Elizabeth laughed. "I appreciate your thoughtfulness." When she returned to where Selena was combing her hair, she asked, "How old are your children?"

"Almost four. Adam is already dropping little hints that he thinks we should have more."

"How do you feel about that?"

"It's not a bad idea at all." She grinned. "I've never found any of Adam's suggestions unreasonable." Her reflection in the mirror doubled the softly dreaming expression she wore. Her gaze met Elizabeth's. "How about you? Do you want more children?"

Elizabeth wasn't sure what to say. "We, uh, we've never discussed it. This pregnancy wasn't exactly planned."

"Very few of them are, you know. But Dan is so obviously proud he's going to be a father. He's adorable . . . and very much in love."

"Why do you say that?"

"Oh, no reason, other than the fact that he can't keep his eyes off you and he's so proud of you. He could hardly wait for us to meet you. I'd say the man is really a goner." She tilted her head slightly, meeting Elizabeth's gaze in the mirror. "You mean you didn't know?" she asked with amused disbelief.

"He's never said," Elizabeth admitted with a slight shrug. "That's the problem with unplanned pregnancies, sometimes—"

"Oho. So for some reason you've decided that Dan did the gentlemanly thing and offered himself to save your honor?"

"Something like that," Elizabeth said, her face flushed.

"Oh, honey, are you ever reading Dan wrong. He's not some naive farm boy, you know. I'm sure he would have worked out some alternative solution if he hadn't wanted to marry you. He's too straightfor-

ward to waste time with game playing. I haven't
known him long, maybe a year, but I found out some
fundamental things about the guy, and you'll never
convince me he married you for any other reason than
that he loves you.''

Hearing it put into words made Elizabeth realize
how much she hoped Selena was right. Perhaps Dan
wasn't trying to make the best out of an awkward situation.

"I don't know much about men," Elizabeth admitted, hoping Selena understood what she meant.

She must have. "You only need to understand one
man—the one you love. And sometimes that takes all
kinds of patience and giving him enough space so he
doesn't feel hemmed in. Adam and I didn't exactly
have the most orthodox of courtships ourselves. For-
tunately I didn't get pregnant before he had come to
terms with our relationship, so I wasn't faced with de-
cisions regarding a family at that point, but I do understand what you're going through." She opened the
door and waited for Elizabeth to join her. "Believe
me, it will be worth the wait. Sooner or later Dan will
admit to you how he feels. You just watch."

The women were laughing when they returned to the
table and Dan was relieved to see they were enjoying
each other's company. They made a study in con-
trasts. Selena was tall and blond; Beth was diminu-
tive and a brunette. But they were both stunning, and
several appreciative glances had followed their so-
journ back to the table.

He reached for Beth's hand once she was seated and stroked it. "Are you feeling tired?" he asked in a quiet voice.

"Not really."

Selena spoke up. "If you'd like some advice, I'd suggest you call it an evening. Believe it or not, being pregnant takes more stamina than most people realize."

Dan agreed quickly and before she knew it, Elizabeth had been bundled up and whisked home. But not before Selena had hugged her and insisted on being notified as soon as the baby arrived.

Later, as Dan went through the exquisitely painful yet addictive back rub, Elizabeth drowsily commented on the evening. "I was really surprised to find Selena Stanford so friendly."

"I told you she was really special."

"And I agree. Of course, knowing that she thinks you walk on water probably influences your opinion of her somewhat."

"You mean because she admires your taste?" he asked with a grin.

"I wonder what she'd think if she knew what a terrific back rub you give?" she asked in a muffled voice, her head buried in her arms.

"Promote me for the presidency?"

"Without a doubt."

Dan thought she was almost asleep and he knew he was in for another restless night when she finally said, "I admire my taste, too."

His hands paused in their movement. "Do you?" he whispered.

She nodded, refusing to look at him.

He pulled the covers up to her shoulders and patted them. "That's a start, anyway."

Chapter Ten

March 3 seemed to be a harbinger of spring. Blue skies and temperate breezes hinted at the warmer weather coming.

Elizabeth woke up with all kinds of energy. She busied herself with the apartment, which took about half an hour because she kept it spotless. Afterward she felt too restless to sit and do handwork.

She decided to strip and rewax the kitchen floor. She needed to feel a sense of accomplishment. Spring housekeeping must be an instinctive feeling buried in all of us, she decided later as she knelt on her hands and knees to scrub.

The exercise felt good. In fact, everything felt good to her. She caught herself humming, experiencing a deep happiness. Everything in her life seemed to be working: her doctor said she was progressing nicely—whatever that meant; she had a handsome, attentive husband and was owned by a cat who tolerated her with amused affection.

What more could anyone ask?

It was only when she stretched out on the bed for her nap later that afternoon that Elizabeth decided she might have overdone her day a little.

She had an ache in her lower back that wouldn't go away. In fact, it seemed to be getting worse. The baby wasn't due for another two weeks at best. The doctor had already commented that the baby was a little smaller than he had expected so near the due date and that she might not deliver for three to four more weeks. She groaned at the thought, then forced herself to relax and get some rest.

Sometime later she woke up, knowing that something was wrong. Her water had broken. She called the doctor immediately and reported what had happened. No, she hadn't noticed contractions as such. Yes, she had some lower back pain, but that seemed to be chronic. Yes, she could get to the hospital within the hour.

So this was it. March 3. Elizabeth recognized the adrenaline flowing through her. She was scared. She was excited. Now was the time to face what had to be done.

But first she had to call Dan.

His secretary put her through to him without delay. Now that the woman recognized her voice, Elizabeth always reached him immediately.

When he answered, she could tell he was distracted, and she wished she had the courage to lie to him. But he'd never forgive her.

"Dan Morgan," he said into the phone.

"Hi, Dan," she began, trying to find a way to soften her news.

"What's wrong?" he demanded. She rarely called him at work, not unless he specifically asked her to call. And that tentative tone of voice was not natural for her.

So much for trying to break the news gently. "My water broke."

"Oh, my God."

"It's nothing to be alarmed about. The doctor wants me at the hospital, so I thought I'd call and—"

"Stay right there. I'll be there in ten minutes."

"Dan, there's no reason for you to leave work. I haven't even started contractions. This being a first baby means I'll probably be there for hours before—"

"Don't move. Don't do anything until I get there."

The phone slammed down and she flinched.

"Oh, dear. He's going to be one of those fathers everybody makes fun of," she informed Misty wryly.

Her bag had been packed for a couple of weeks, so all Elizabeth had to do was to change into something to wear to the hospital and wait for Dan to arrive.

He burst into the apartment a short time later and came to an abrupt stop when he found her waiting patiently for him in the overstuffed chair by the sofa.

"You okay?"

"I'm fine. You made good time."

"I took a cab. It was faster than getting the car out."

She stood up and he immediately wrapped his arm around her. "My legs are still in good working order. Are you ready to go?"

"The cab's waiting."

"Would you mind getting my suitcase? It's in the closet."

He disappeared into the bedroom and returned in less than a minute with her bag. Keeping a close hold on her, Dan escorted Elizabeth out of the apartment, made sure the door was locked, then took her down the elevator to the waiting cab.

"Are you sure you're okay?" he asked again while the cab took them across town.

"I'm fine."

"Are you in any pain?"

Not the kind of pain she had expected. Her lower back felt as though it were going to snap in two, but she saw no point in mentioning it.

Once again the hospital employees seemed to know exactly what needed to be done with the minimum amount of fuss. Dr. Fitzgerald was there by the time she was undressed and in bed.

When he was through with his examination he sat down beside her on the bed and took her hand. "I noticed your husband referred to you as Beth. Would you mind if I call you that?"

His voice sounded very gentle and soothing, but the serious expression in his eyes worried her. "Of course not."

He sat there for a moment, studying her in silence.

"There's something wrong, isn't there?" she finally asked.

"We don't know why these things happen, Beth. There never seems to be an understandable reason, and it seldom helps to analyze deeply."

"I'm going to lose the baby."

"Not if I can help it. But I can't make any guarantees. I'm going to do the best I can and I'm counting on you to do the same."

All Beth could think about at the moment was Dan. He wanted the baby. He married her for the baby. And now they might lose it.

"I need your permission to do a cesarean section. At the moment that seems to be the safest thing for both you and the baby."

"Whatever you want to do."

"Fine. I'll have the nurse in here in a few moments and give you a shot to relax you before surgery." He squeezed her hand and stood up.

"Are you going to tell Dan?"

"Of course. And we'll hope for the best. But sometimes, Beth, it's better to be prepared for the worst."

She lay there after the door closed, listening for voices, but all she heard were muffled sounds.

The pain seemed to be surrounding her, crowding down on her so that she could scarcely breathe. Tears trickled down her cheeks. Her baby. Her beautiful, longed-for baby.

The door opened and the nurse came in. Before the door slowly swung shut again she heard Dan's voice.

"Don't let anything happen to Beth, Doctor. I know you're doing your best, but if there's a choice and you can only save one of them, don't allow Beth to die, do you hear me? We can have other children. No one can replace her."

She heard the doctor answer in a soothing voice. "We're going to do our damnedest to save them both, but I understand how you feel, Dan. Believe me, you aren't alone. She's your wife, and you love her."

"Of course I love her. I waited for years to find her, and then when I did, I managed to get her pregnant and jeopardize her life!"

"You didn't get her pregnant without some assistance from her, you know. Don't blame yourself, okay?"

Beth could no longer hear them, but she would never forget Dan's words.

I've waited for years to find her. I love her. I've waited for years to find her. I love her.

He was waiting in the hallway when they wheeled her into surgery. The shot had made her very drowsy and she sleepily smiled at him.

She was too pale, Dan decided. Her black hair framed her face, her dark, delicate brows her only color. He took her hand and walked beside her. When he had to let go he kissed her palm and gently laid her hand down again.

* * *

Beth's dreams were strange and disjointed. Voices and singing kept weaving in and out of her consciousness. She felt different—lighter, full of energy, filled with joy.

Dan loves me. He loves me . . . loves me . . . loves . . .

"Beth?"

Her eyes opened slowly and she fought to focus on the shadowy figure beside her. Her back no longer hurt, but she felt a heaviness on her stomach that hadn't been there earlier.

The baby must have gained so much weight that—

The baby?

"The baby. . ." she whispered through dry lips. She managed to focus on Dan and notice that strain had drawn lines down his face she'd never seen before.

"I don't know. They're still working with him."

"Him?"

He smiled slightly. "You were right. It's a little boy."

"Have you talked with the doctor?"

"He's turned him over to the pediatrics people. The baby is small, Beth, and they had trouble getting him to breathe."

She could feel the tears running down her cheeks once again. "I'm sorry," she whispered.

"Oh, God, love, so am I. So sorry that I've put you through so much pain. I'm sorry about so many things."

She saw the moisture in his eyes. "I'm sorry our son is having a rough time. But we don't have to give up hope."

He nodded. "I don't intend to, believe me. You said yourself he's a scrapper. He'll hang in there if at all possible—I'm sure of it." He leaned over and kissed her on the forehead. "Get some sleep. I'll see you in the morning."

"Dan?"

"Yes, love."

"Thank you for being with me. I'll never forget how much you've done for me."

Fear gripped him at her remark. She sounded as though she were saying goodbye. The doctor had warned him that she would be weak. She'd lost a lot of blood. Neither she nor the baby were out of the woods yet. Not by a long shot.

"Get some rest," he repeated. "I'll see you in the morning."

Dan stepped out into the hallway and sighed. The past few hours had been some of the worst he had ever spent. He wasn't sure at the moment if he was ready to face what the future might bring.

The apartment seemed empty when he got back. Misty greeted him at the door, looking behind him as though wondering what he'd done with Beth.

"She's at the hospital," he explained, no longer feeling ridiculous to be talking to an animal. Misty seemed to understand everything that was said to her. She immediately left the door and went over and sat by her empty bowl.

"I know. It's time to eat. Thanks for reminding me. We both need to keep up our strength."

The doctor had convinced him to go home and get some rest. He was right. He'd be no good to anybody if he didn't take care of himself.

After feeding Misty, Dan stared into the refrigerator blankly. Beth had left a salad and roast. Forcing himself, he ate, cleaned up his dishes and went to bed.

He never noticed the brightly shining, newly waxed floor.

"Your wife is running a fever this morning, Mr. Morgan," the day nurse informed him. "The baby is holding his own. We're keeping him in an incubator, which is standard procedure for a child that small."

"Has the doctor been in this morning?"

"Oh, yes. He was in quite early. He's prescribed medication for Mrs. Morgan to clear up the infection."

"May I see her?"

"Certainly. She may be asleep, though. The pain medication that's standard after surgery has kept her drowsy, which is just as well. Her body needs time to heal."

Dan opened the door and peered into the shadowed room. The blinds and drapes were closed.

She lay there so still. He couldn't shake off the feeling of desolation that swept over him when he saw her.

He sat down in the chair by the bed and her eyes opened.

"Hello," he offered.

"I thought I was dreaming."

"About what?"

"You. I thought I dreamed you were here."

"I just walked in."

She smiled. "Maybe my dream brought you here."

"Sounds possible to me."

He stood up and moved closer, taking her hand. "How do you feel?"

"Like I'm floating several inches off the bed. Whatever those shots are they're giving me, they're powerful." She studied his sober expression. "Have you seen the baby?"

"Not since last night."

"What does he look like?"

Dan thought a moment. "It's hard to tell. He looked so damned small!"

"Could you tell the color of his hair?"

"It looked dark, like yours."

"And eyes?"

"No. He never opened them."

"Have you decided on a name yet?"

"Have you?"

"Would you mind if we named him after you? We could call him Danny."

"If that's what you want."

"Yes." Her eyes closed briefly and he could see the struggle she had opening them.

"Don't fight it, love. Let the medication have it's effect."

"You've been calling me that since you brought me in."

"Calling you what?"

"'Love.'"

He didn't think he could talk around the lump in his throat. "I've always thought of you as my love," he admitted.

"But you never told me."

"No."

"Why not?"

"Because I didn't think you'd want to hear it."

She smiled. "Well, what do you know. The great Dan Morgan is finally wrong about something."

She sounded slightly inebriated and he almost laughed. "I take that to mean you wanted to hear it."

"It would have been nice all that time when I felt so fat and ugly."

"You were never fat and ugly. You have always been a beautiful woman, and I love you to distraction."

"I'm so glad." She sighed with contentment. "I love you, too."

For a moment he thought he'd imagined the words. She said them so casually. His eyes met hers and he saw the tender light in them that he had noticed more than once.

"Do you, Beth? Do you, really?"

"Of course. How could I help but love you? You're one of the most wonderful men in the world."

"Hold that thought, love, until you get out of here. I have a hunch I'd like to pursue this conversation when you've recovered a little more." He could feel the blood rushing through his body.

"Does that mean you want to make love to me?" she asked with drowsy interest.

Dan caught himself looking over his shoulder to make sure one of the nurses hadn't walked into the room. "The thought has crossed my mind on more than one occasion since I first met you."

"You hid it well, then. You never seemed to show that much interest in me."

"That's all you know. I've had a rough time keeping my hands off you for months."

The smile she gave him was dazzling. "I'm delighted to hear it." He smiled back and they looked at each other in silence for a few moments.

Then he squeezed her hand. "Go back to sleep. You probably won't remember a single word of this conversation later."

"Don't count on it. I've gotten the distinct impression you intend to lose some of that restraint you've been practicing. I'll do all I can to help you toss it out the window when I get home."

"I can hardly wait."

He watched as her eyes closed again and he continued to hold her hand until her even breathing convinced him she was sound asleep once more.

Then he tiptoed out of the room. He wanted to go visit Danny and give his son a pep talk about fighting and holding on.

When the phone rang the first time Dan groggily thought it was the alarm and reached over to the nightstand for the switch to turn it off. By the second ring he was wide-awake, aware that when the phone rang at four in the morning, it was rarely good news.

"This is Riverside General Hospital, Mr. Morgan," a feminine voice said. "The doctor thought you'd want to know that your son is having some difficulties breathing and that you might want to be here."

"I'm on my way," Dan said. He was dressed and going out the door within minutes.

When he arrived on the floor, the nurse assured him that everything possible was being done. They had not disturbed Beth, so Dan stayed out in the hallway, waiting for word, praying that the tiny baby made it.

He didn't know how much time passed before the young pediatrician in charge joined him.

"He's doing much better now. I'm sorry to have awakened you this morning."

"I'm glad you did."

"He's tenacious—I'll give him that. Let's hope he doesn't give us another scare like that one."

"Amen," Dan agreed. "Have you told my wife?"

"Not yet."

"I don't see any need to alarm her at this point, do you? Particularly if he's through the crisis."

"I'll leave that to your judgment, Mr. Morgan."

The men shook hands briefly and Dan walked down to Beth's room.

Weak sunlight filtered through the window. Her color was much better and she seemed to be resting. He stood watching her for a moment before he had to go back home to clean up.

Her eyes opened and she saw him. "You're here early, aren't you?"

He smiled. "I missed you."

She held out her hand, and he stepped closer to the bed and took it. Studying him in the early-morning light, she frowned slightly. "You haven't shaved."

"It's the new look, didn't you know?" He leaned over and kissed her.

She placed her hand on his cheek and rubbed it lightly. "Whatever you say," she responded doubtfully.

"Has the doctor said when you'll be able to go home?"

"Not until I quit running this stupid fever."

"How about Danny?"

"That depends on how fast he gains his weight. They told me last night he's eating well. In fact, I'm supposed to be able to feed him this morning."

He hoped that nothing had changed in that respect.

"I called a realtor yesterday to start looking for a place upstate. But I'd rather wait until you're up to looking with me."

"Are you sure that's what you want?"

"More than anything else." He leaned over and kissed her again. "I'll be back tonight. Get well in a hurry, love. I want you home."

She watched him leave the room with a slight frown on her face. Something was bothering him, but she supposed she'd have to wait until he was ready to tell her.

Her husband could be stubborn on occasion, she'd discovered during the past months. She smiled. Otherwise he would never have found her last fall. Beth shifted, trying to get comfortable. There were worse traits, she supposed, than stubbornness.

Chapter Eleven

Elizabeth felt as though she'd been away from the apartment for a month, rather than ten days. She feasted on the familiar color scheme of the bedroom and enjoyed the feeling of being home.

Danny slept peacefully in his crib in an alcove of the bedroom.

The hospital staff was amazed at the progress he'd made. After a wobbly first few days, he started gaining strength as well as weight. Earlier the doctor had warned her that Danny might need to stay at the hospital when she was discharged, but by the time they had her temperature back to normal, both of them were pronounced ready to greet the world.

Dan came out of the bathroom and crawled into bed with her. "At last," he muttered, holding her close. "I've got you where I want you."

She turned a little gingerly, still aware of her incision, and hugged him. "No wonder you're such a success. You have marvelous ideas."

"Is Danny all right?"

"Fine. Ate like a little pig and went off to sleep."

"I think he's going to have your eyes."

"All newborns' eyes are blue."

"Maybe they won't change."

"He's got your features."

"A nice mix."

He kissed her lightly, felt the warmth and softness of her mouth and groaned. Deepening the kiss, Dan held her closer, enjoying having her in his arms once more.

Dan's touch seemed to set off tiny explosions deep within Elizabeth, like depth charges, causing a chain reaction of heat to race through her.

Eventually he drew away, drawing a deep breath. "I seem to have lost all that restraint I've been hanging on to." He edged away from her slightly. "You go to my head."

Elizabeth fit her body to his in the sleeping position that had become natural to her. "It's good to be home."

Dan agreed, but he had forgotten how strongly she affected him, being there in bed with him.

He forced himself to think of other things, until he finally fell asleep with Beth curled up beside him, his son resting nearby.

* * *

"Beth?" Dan called.

"I'm in here," she replied, carrying Danny out of the bedroom. "What are you doing home?"

"Just as I suspected," he said without expression. "While I'm off slaving all day, trying to support your extravagant tastes, you're spending time with another man."

He lifted Danny from her shoulder and cuddled him under his chin.

"I wouldn't exactly consider him a man, but he's certainly growing," Elizabeth admitted. "So why are you home?"

"You aren't pleased to see me?" he asked.

She grinned. He knew better. During the past two months she had made it clear that she enjoyed being with him, sharing his home and the care of his son. In short, there was no doubt that he was aware of her feelings for him.

"I am delighted to see you, Mr. Morgan. Absolutely delighted. To what do I owe this unexpected treat?"

"How about taking a ride with me? I think the realtor may have found something."

Elizabeth hadn't realized he'd been actively looking for a home for them. After being up with a baby all hours of the night, Dan could easily have changed his mind about a wife and child. She knew better, of course. He'd had too many opportunities to shy away from the situation if he'd wished.

For a man who'd been a bachelor a short year before, Dan had taken to fatherhood with amazing speed.

"Let me get some of Danny's things together."

They were on their way north within the hour.

"I know this is going to sound strange," Dan said quietly after they got away from the heavier traffic, "but I dreamed about a house last night. Don't ask me why. But I could practically draw the house plans the dream was so clear. The house sat back from a winding street, up on a hill, with several trees that looked as if they'd always been there." He seemed to be remembering more as he talked. "The walkway to the front door was made of bricks laid in an intricate pattern, and a large bay window was by the front door, so that you could see inside to a comfortable room with a fireplace. The furniture reminded me of the kind we had when I was growing up—sturdy, almost childproof."

He glanced at Beth. "Now that I think of it, you were in the dream."

"Oh? Doing what?"

"You were just there, as I recall. There were children around. I remember that."

She looked down at the baby in her arms, placidly sleeping. Children, not just one. Glancing up at Dan once more, she couldn't help but remember—

"I guess the weird thing about it is that I rarely remember dreams. Do you?"

She thought of her recurring dream about Philip. "Not lately. I used to dream all the time, though."

"Good dreams?"

"Not particularly."

The realtor had given them directions to the house they were to view, agreeing to meet them there.

Elizabeth felt as though what was happening wasn't real. She'd gone through the previous months, waiting for the baby's arrival, deliberately pushing the future away. Suddenly the future had arrived and she wasn't at all sure she was ready for it.

Following the directions, they turned onto a narrow street that began to wind upward around a hill.

"Eight-seventeen. There it is," Dan began, then fell silent.

The house was set back from the winding street on a hillside. A large bay window was located by the front door. When they pulled into the driveway behind the realtor's car, they saw him waiting for them on the brick walkway that led to the front door—a brick walkway with an intricate design.

"I don't believe this," Dan muttered.

He helped Elizabeth out of the car. He knew before they reached the front door what he would see through the bay window. A large fireplace with bookshelves on either side dominated one wall. He was relieved to find the room empty of furniture. At least something was different from his dream.

They wandered through the house in silence. Elizabeth couldn't get over how familiar it seemed to her. There were no secrets. She knew which doors led to the basement, to the pantry, the linen closet, the master bedroom. She gazed out of one of the windows that faced the back. A sloping lawn covered with large trees ended at a high wooden fence. A safe place for children to play.

Children. She looked down at Danny once more. Was it possible he was going to have someone to play with?

The realtor did his work well. He pointed out specifics, but made no effort to coerce. Perhaps he realized he didn't need to push. When Elizabeth went back downstairs Dan was waiting in the hallway. He looked a little pale.

"What do you think?" he asked in a low voice.

"It's a dream house, wouldn't you say?"

If anything, his color faded even more.

"It's not funny, Beth. The last time I felt this way I—"

She waited, but he seemed to be at a loss for words.

"You what, Dan?"

"I was remembering the night I met you at Ryan's and how I felt when I first saw you. You seemed so familiar, as though I'd known you for years but had lost touch with you." He shook his head a little, as though bewildered. "And now this house. I don't understand."

"Neither do I."

"Do you feel it?"

"I feel a sense of familiarity. Is that what you mean?"

"Yes. I suppose that's as good a description as any. We're going to buy it, aren't we?" he asked thoughtfully.

"If you feel that we can afford it."

"That's the irony of it. This house has been vacant for over a year, according to the realtor. The people who own it moved to the West Coast and they've had trouble selling it because of its size." He looked up the curving staircase. "This house is too big for three of us. The realtor had already mentioned that to me, but it was a good location and the price is excellent, so he thought it worth mentioning."

"Maybe we'll have to produce a family to fill it," she suggested with a slight smile.

Dan remembered the problems of her last pregnancy. "No. It's too dangerous."

"We'll see." She turned away and started for the front door, where the realtor had discreetly disappeared earlier. Pausing, she glanced over her shoulder. "What do you think? Shall we make an offer?"

"For some reason, I don't feel as though we have a choice. It looks as though we're home, love."

By the time they returned to the apartment they were both excited, laughing at how easily everything had fallen into place. Closing could be scheduled in a few short weeks. It would take them that long to decide what furniture they wanted to keep and move and what needed to be purchased for the new home.

"Don't you think you should keep the apartment in Manhattan, in case you need to stay in town occasionally?"

"If I have to stay in town, I'll get a room at a hotel and insist that my wife join me. No. I don't intend to keep the apartment."

They talked through dinner, through Danny's feeding, and when Elizabeth went in to take her shower Dan followed her in to make a suggestion, only to stop when he realized what he had done.

She had reached into the shower to adjust the water temperature, when she heard his voice and looked over her shoulder.

He hadn't meant to invade her privacy. He'd been following her around the apartment all evening while she took care of things, and out of habit had continued to do so.

She stood there, slender once again, without anything hiding her from him. Except for their first evening together, he'd never seen her completely unclothed. That had been almost a year ago.

For a brief moment the events of that year flashed through his mind: the months of trying to forget her, then searching to find out who she was; finding her and discovering she was pregnant with his baby; convincing her to marry him; visiting in her home; having her move in with him; seeing her in pain at the time of delivery; fearing that he was going to lose her.

In a few short months she had become an integral part of his life and yet he'd been unable to express his love for her physically.

Elizabeth could feel a warm flush cover her body as Dan stood there, staring at her. She didn't know why she should be embarrassed. He was her husband, after all. He'd been very considerate, never pushing for physical intimacy after Danny's birth.

Slowly she turned toward him. "I'm sorry. I didn't hear what you said."

"I've forgotten," he mumbled, stepping into the room and closing the door. He touched a wisp of hair that curled before her ear. "You are so beautiful," he whispered, "and I love you more than I thought it possible to love anyone."

She began to unbutton his shirt. "The shower's big enough for two. Think we should do our part to help conserve water?"

He slid his hands on either side of her neck, his thumbs tilting her chin until he could touch her mouth with his.

She'd become addicted to his kisses. He was always so gentle. Tonight he was even more so, as though waiting for her to pull away. Elizabeth had no intention of pulling away.

The past year had taught her a great deal—about herself, her perception of the world and the people with whom she came into contact. She wasn't the same person who had gone to Ryan Davidson's party to pretend for a few hours that she was someone else. Elizabeth had gotten in touch with who she was and begun to remove the barriers she'd erected so many years before—just in time for Dan Morgan to come striding into her life.

She wanted him in every way a woman could want a man—as her companion, as her partner, as her lover, as the father of her children.

His shirt hung open and she tugged at the shoulders, trying to remove it. Dan reluctantly let go of her long enough to shrug out of his shirt. With economical movements he removed the rest of his clothing and stood there before her, a question in his eyes.

"I love you, Dan," she said quietly.

He felt his knees quiver slightly. How long had he waited to see that look of love and trust in her eyes? He reached behind her and opened the shower door. "After you, milady."

There wasn't much room, but the cramped quarters didn't seem to bother them. Dan took his time carefully covering Beth with soap, turning her away from him to lovingly stroke her back.

"I've missed getting to massage your back," he offered once she had rinsed and started to cover his broad shoulders with suds.

"I can't imagine why. I'm sure you found it quite tedious."

"Hardly. It was the only time I could trust myself to touch you."

She tugged at him slightly to turn. Once he was facing her she knew how affected he was by their closeness. "Can you trust yourself to touch me now?"

"Not if I have to walk away once we're through with our shower."

"You don't ever have to walk away from me, Dan."

"You know that I love you, don't you?"

"Yes. You taught me what love is all about. It isn't a taking—it's giving . . . and sharing . . . and trusting."

"And you trust me?"

"Yes."

"Despite what happened our first evening together?"

"Aren't you ever going to forgive yourself for that? I was a willing participant."

He pulled her close to him. "Hmmmmm, so you were." He began to plant small kisses along her jaw, up her cheek, until he found her mouth.

His kiss was no longer gentle. A surge of possessiveness swept over him. He'd campaigned long and hard to win her. Dan couldn't believe the waiting was over.

They took their time drying each other, stopping to kiss and caress each other. Then Dan picked her up and carried her into the bedroom, placing her on the bed. The night-light glowed nearby, but Dan couldn't see her expression as he stretched out beside her.

She placed her hand on his chest, rubbing it across the muscled surface. Elizabeth could feel the heat emanating from his body.

Any fears she might have had were gone. She loved this man and wanted to be a part of him.

Soft touches became trembling caresses. Whispered phrases joined breathless pleas and muffled moans of pleasure. Even in the midst of their loving passion, they were aware of the baby close by, the baby who had brought them together in what had become a strange enchantment.

Epilogue

Do you intend to teach next year?" Janine asked, watching Beth efficiently preparing dinner in her large, country kitchen.

Beth glanced down at her as yet flat abdomen and smiled. "Good question. We haven't discussed it."

"It seems to me there're several things you haven't discussed," Janine offered tartly. "Such as overpopulation."

Beth laughed. "I don't think our family is going to create world-wide famine, do you?"

"But you had such a tough time that first time. How can you forget?"

"I've never forgotten. But I didn't have any trouble with the other two, remember?"

"But four children, Beth," she chided. "Nobody has that many children in today's world. It just isn't done."

"It is in our family."

The back door flew open and a dark-haired, blue-eyed boy of eight years or so paused in the doorway. "When are we eating, Mom?"

Beth glanced around at him, casually inspecting the dirt on his jeans and the stain on his shirt. "It will be another hour, Danny. You'll have time to get bathed and cleaned up."

"Oh, Mom, do I have to?"

She nodded toward Janine. "We have company tonight."

Janine looked over at the boy and winked. He reluctantly grinned in response.

"Where are Amy and Melissa?" Beth asked.

"They're outside pestering Mark." In his most adult voice he said, "He isn't used to girls, Mom. I wish you'd make them behave."

"What are they doing?"

"Amy keeps wanting to put bandages on him. She says she's going to be a doctor. And Melissa keeps trying to read to him."

Janine raised a brow slightly. "Melissa can read?"

"Well, she thinks she can." Danny shrugged. "She's pretty good at talking about the pictures for a three-year-old," he admitted from his advanced years.

"Why don't you have the girls come in and get cleaned up, too? Maybe then they'll leave your friend Mark alone."

"I can try," he said with a resigned expression, disappearing from view once again.

"How long has Amy been planning to be a doctor?" Janine asked with a grin.

"Since the time we had to rush Danny in for stitches after he fell. She was very impressed with all the goings-on."

"But she's only seven. She could always change her mind."

"Of course."

Janine continued to watch her friend, taking in the changes in her. She was still slender—having children didn't seem to affect Beth's weight. Her hair was much shorter now. It was cut in a cap of curls around her head, making her look almost as young as her son, whose mop of black hair always seemed to need a brush.

"What does Dan think?"

"About what?"

"Your pregnancy, Beth. That was what we were discussing before Danny the whirlwind arrived."

"Oh. Well, you know Dan—"

"Not the way you do. Obviously."

They laughed, enjoying the camaraderie.

"He seems to revel in the family. He's hired some good management people, so he doesn't spend as much time in Manhattan as he did. He insists he'd just as soon be here with the kids while I teach, since I only have classes two days a week. He didn't like having a live-in housekeeper." Her face flushed a little at the memory. "He said she cramped his style."

"I can imagine."

"Of course I have plenty of help. Gladys comes in each morning and does the heavy cleaning." She placed a casserole in the oven. "There, that should do it. Want to join the men in the other room?"

Janine glanced at the door into the hallway. "In a moment. I, uh, there's something I wanted to talk to you about."

"Sure."

Beth pulled up another bar stool and sat down beside Janine.

"Ryan has asked me to marry him."

"You're kidding me!"

"I know. I can't believe it, either. And the problem is, I don't know what to say to him."

"You've been in love with him for years. What's there to think about?"

"You...and Dan...and your family. I'm not at all sure I could handle all of this. I'm damned good at what I do, but it has nothing to do with domesticity."

"Come on, Janine. Ryan has known you long enough to understand that."

"But he may expect me to change. You changed."

Beth glanced out the window to make sure the children were getting ready to come inside. Amy was mothering Melissa as usual and Melissa was doing a better job of tolerating her than usual. Perhaps it was going to be a quiet evening after all.

"I changed because this is what I want, Janine. Not because Dan asked me to."

"But didn't you feel the pressure?"

"No. I'm not sure I know how to explain this, but I'll try. Dan and I belong together...in this house... with a large family. We've known that from the beginning."

"You mean like fate, or something?"

"It was just a feeling we had. I had let my early life warp me a little and the relationship with Philip didn't help. But meeting Dan brought my life into a sharper focus and I realized what I was doing to myself by constantly clinging to the hurts of the past. Once I let go, I was free to enjoy life and all it offered."

"And you feel being a wife and mother is the end-all and be-all of existence?"

"Of course not. I still teach, which I love, but my horizons have broadened to include Dan and the children. Everyone is different, Janine. Don't try to fit yourself into a mold. Be honest with Ryan. Tell him of your concerns. You might be surprised to discover he's not interested in a family, either. You have a good relationship now. Marriage will only give you an opportunity to improve on it."

"Aren't you two ever going to join us?" Dan slid his arms around Beth from behind and hugged her around the middle. "Ryan and I are totally bored with each other's company."

"Now that I'll never believe," Beth said, resting her head for a moment against his shoulder.

"What if I said I missed you?" he whispered.

"I might be persuaded to believe that."

"What would it take to convince you?"

"I swear you two act like a couple of newlyweds," Janine complained good-naturedly.

Dan laughed, a relaxed, happy sound that danced around the room.

"What's so funny?" Ryan asked, leaning against the doorjamb, his hands in his pockets.

"Never mind," Beth responded, sitting up and looking around at Ryan. "Would you guys like something else to drink? Dinner should be ready in thirty minutes or so."

"Not me," Dan responded. "Unless you have some lemonade made." He grinned at Ryan. "I can't handle the hard stuff anymore. Must be out of the habit."

"I know what you mean. When I developed that ulcer I learned not to drink anything stronger than milk." He looked over at Beth. "I understand congratulations are in order."

Her gaze met Dan's and she formed the words, "Loud mouth." He just grinned, totally unabashed.

"That's right."

"You seem to be trying to rebuild the economy single-handedly. Glad it's you and not me. I couldn't handle being tied down. Guess I'm too used to traveling without having to worry about anything more than how soon I need to get to the airport."

Beth exchanged a significant glance with Janine.

"That doesn't mean I don't intend to spoil your kids rotten, though," Ryan continued. "I think I'll go see what they're up to out there."

He sauntered over to the back door and stepped outside. Janine nodded slightly at Beth and said,

"Think I'll join you, Ryan, love. There's something I wanted to tell you."

"Ah, alone at last," Dan whispered, gathering Beth into his arms once more. She giggled at the lecherous tone of voice.

"For all of two minutes, max."

"Hmmm. In that case, I'll just stand here and nibble a little before dinner." He kissed her under her ear, then took little nips along her neck.

"Dan?"

"Hmmm?"

"Are you sorry about the baby?"

He jerked away as though she had struck him. "Sorry? Are you kidding? Danny and I have to see about evening up the numbers around here." He leaned back, keeping his arms around her so that he could see her face. "Are you?"

"Of course not."

"One more should fill the remaining bedroom upstairs."

"Yes," she agreed with a smile.

"I've enjoyed living here with you, Mrs. Morgan."

"Time seems to have flown by, hasn't it?"

"I suppose, in one sense. In another way, I feel that I've always been with you and that I always will be with you. Kinda strange, I know."

"I feel the same way. I'm glad we found each other when we did."

"Me, too. It was getting a little lonely, waiting around. Especially when I didn't even realize what I was waiting for."

"Until Ryan's party."

"Yeah. Until the night of Ryan's party."

They walked to the back door, arms around each other, and watched their family entertaining their guests.

ATTRACTIVE, SPACE SAVING BOOK RACK

Display your most prized novels on this handsome and sturdy book rack. The hand-rubbed walnut finish will blend into your library decor with quiet elegance, providing a practical organizer for your favorite hard- or soft-covered books.

Only $9.95

Approximately 16" x 8" when assembled

Assembles in seconds!

To order, rush your name, address and zip code, along with a check or money order for $10.70* ($9.95 plus 75¢ postage and handling) payable to *Silhouette Books.*

Silhouette Books
Book Rack Offer
901 Fuhrmann Blvd.
P.O. Box 1325
Buffalo, NY 14269-1325

Offer not available in Canada.

BKR-2R

*New York residents add appropriate sales tax.

Silhouette ❦ *Romance*

COMING NEXT MONTH

IT TAKES A THIEF—Rita Rainville
When Dani Clayton broke into the wrong office at the wrong casino, she was caught—by devastating Rafe Sutherland. Dani was determined to get to the right place; Rafe was determined to keep her out. Two such strong-willed people just *had* to fall in love.

A PEARL BEYOND PRICE—Lucy Gordon
Not even the barriers from their pasts could prevent the sparks that flew between Renato and Lynette. Renato was a hard man—would he ever understand the pricelessness of Lynette's love?

IN HOT PURSUIT—Pepper Adams
Secret Service Agent J. P. Tucker had been trailing Maggie Ryan for weeks. But it wasn't until after he'd rescued her from kidnappers and counterfeiters, and was chased all over the state, that he realized there was more to shy Maggie than met the eye!

HIGH RIDER—Olivia Ferrell
Rodeo clown Rama Daniels wanted a stable home life, and she was sure she couldn't have one with Barc Lawson. Barc was a rodeo rider, a nomad. Though he professed he was ready to settle down, Rama knew rodeo was in his blood. Could he ever convince her otherwise?

HEARTS ON FIRE—Brenda Trent
Glenna Johnson had always wanted to be a firefighter, and now she had her chance. She knew she could put out the fires, but could she handle the burning glances of station captain Reid Shelden?

THE LEOPARD TREE—Valerie Parv
Her first UFO! Tanith had always wanted to see one, and now she had. But was the mysterious, compelling stranger who arrived with it alien or human? Evidence said alien, but her heart said he was very much a man.

AVAILABLE THIS MONTH: